Happy as the Grass Was Green

Happy as the Grass Was Green

By
Merle Good

HERALD PRESS, SCOTTDALE, PENNSYLVANIA

1

The things they say about the trains not really wanting passengers are true. If the trains are running, they're likely to be running late. Late, noisy, and dirty. And smelly. Half-empty cups of soft drink that travelers paid a fortune for and left abandoned among the luggage, crumpled newspapers, and broken seats. The railroad's going out of business.

Jim and I sit alone, staring at the late afternoon New Jersey countryside as the train hurries toward Pennsylvania. Neither of us has spoken since the train crawled from the dark station hours ago. Jim never talks much. Today he speaks not a word. A shadow of death hangs in the filthy car about us and Jim watches it with narrow eyes. Suspiciously. His jaw is set and his fingers dig into each other as he sees the world go by. His ruffled charcoal hair falls down all over his dirty face.

Jim doesn't move. He doesn't speak. I wonder if he's even breathing. It's as though his heart has frozen in mid-beat and Jim's whole young life is standing mute.

I offer him a cigarette. He doesn't notice. So I light one myself. I haven't smoked so much tobacco since I entered college. But the smoke is good. It's like a friend on a cold late bloody October afternoon.

Big John is dead. I know that's far out, but it's true. Jim's own twin brother — dead. Killed by the cops last night. And Jim and I are going home to bury him.

I get up and go back to the men's room in the next car. The place is freezing and the toilet's broken, the frosted glass cracked and dirty. I stand watching the blur of New Jersey's flat fields and wonder why in the world I volunteered to come along with Jim. I haven't been to Pennsylvania for years, not since Grandmom died in Philadelphia. I'm not very good at mixing with the Establishment types either, especially not at funerals. I should have stayed in New York to help the Revolution. Now that three students are dead, the place has got to burn. The cops aren't going to get away with this. They act as though human life has a negotiable price tag. Wow.

So why'd I come with Jim? I don't quite know. I always liked Big John. He was a little kid, much smaller than his twin. Little kid with a big nose. Big nose and big voice. You could hear Big John at every demonstration, shouting at the cops and keeping up the morale when things got tough. I remember once when we stood in the cold rain for three days and nights, protesting that nuclear installation on the upper campus — it was Big John who kept us there with his big voice, singing and shouting. And now his voice is gone.

I think that's why I've come. I want to make sure they bury Big John right. He would appreciate it.

Jim says his folks are Mennonite farmers. Big John a Mennonite! That *is* far out. I don't know anything about Mennonites except they drive horse and buggies and they live in something like monasteries. And to think that's where Big John grew up! And that's where they'll bury him.

I admit I'm a little scared. Closing down the administration building for eight days. And then in the middle of the night they turn the cops loose. Without warning. It's the scene we prepared for all these months. But it's bad. Very bad. Kids waking up with broken skulls, beat in as they lay there. Screaming to hit the fire escapes and throw back the tear gas. My girl kicks a cop in the stomach and sends him flying down the stairs. And then I hear Big John. His voice fills the room with the shout of battle. "The Revolution has come, brothers and sisters," he roars. And to the cops, "Good morning, pigs. Thought you'd catch us by surprise, did you? Well, let it be said for one and all that we are the people and the only way for the powers of darkness to drag us out of here is to kill us first!"

And then Big John began to sing. It's like a record on my brain. Kids fighting hand to hand with cops their own age, sweating hate and blood with morning sneaking in. And singing calmly through it all was little Big John. But suddenly the singing stopped.

And now the train is taking us to bury him in some Pennsylvania Mennonite monastery. And that's a different scene. I feel alone. Alone and afraid.

Jim sits staring as before. Lost in silent grief. He and John never agreed on politics. But that didn't keep them from being brothers. The friend kind of brothers. John roomed with me but lived more with Jim. Sometimes I thought they were escaping together. From what, I didn't know.

The train slows. A gust of cold air chasing him, the conductor announces Philadelphia. So we're in Pennsylvania. Good old city for brothers of love. The buildings stand like gray, unshaven men along the tracks, waiting for the sun to go away so that they can sleep.

"Eric."

"Yeah, Jim," I say, watching the unshaven old men.

"Eric, I wonder how they'll bury John," Jim says.

"Why did you say that?" I ask.

"Because." He hasn't moved. "I bet they'll shave him and cut his hair for the funeral."

"Really?" The bearded men along the tracks begin to move again and we are on our way once more.

"I wouldn't even be surprised if they dress him in one of his old plain suits," Jim says.

"What are they?" I ask.

"Something like a Nehru jacket. Only it's not classy. It's the conservative way of dressing in my home community. They do it for nonconformity."

"You wore one?"

"Sure. John and I both wore them. Man, you should have seen us before we went to college." A trace of a smile softens Jim's face. "See, we grew up in this small Mennonite farming community and we were the squarest bunch of guys you ever saw. Well, not quite the squarest. We didn't have a lot of money. We weren't what you'd call middle American. We were a small, almost pitiful subculture."

I'm glad Jim is starting to talk. It'll take his mind off things. "How did you ever get to the city, Jim?" I ask.

"John had this friend who went to a small college near Pittsburgh. When he found out we were interested in going, he told us about all the schools he knew. So we both decided to apply to the best and biggest. And somehow we were both accepted."

"Did you always want to be a lawyer, Jim?"

"No. No, I had no idea what I wanted. John wanted to be a doctor."

"A doctor." I can't help laughing.

"Yeah, he was always ambitious," Jim says. "I thought he'd really be a doctor. He liked people so much. And people liked him. Well, you know that. Even at home he was a sort of hero. It used to make me mad."

"So why'd he switch to political science?"

Jim smiles before he answers. "I think it was the people. To him the country was rotting at the seams and the only way to really change things was through politics. So he went the whole way. We disagreed, of course."

I nod. Many were the times Jim had come to our room to change his brother's mind. But Big John just sat and laughed at him. They were good at arguing.

The train is moving faster now. An old woman has curled up across several seats and sleeps with her head hanging into the aisle, swinging back and forth in rhythm to the train, her mouth noisy with her breathing. I wish that I could rest. But mystery keeps me staring out across the Pennsylvania hills. Mystery of

9

death. And mystery of reaching out to touch things that can't be touched.

"I didn't tell Pop on the phone how John died," Jim says. "It would kill him and Mother if they would ever find out."

"Don't you suppose they heard it on the news?" I ask.

"No. They don't have radio or television."

"You're kidding."

"No, I'm not." Jim begins to rub his hands the way he does when he gets uptight. "No, we never had any."

"No newspaper either?"

"Oh, boy — how'd I forget? Sure they get the newspaper. Do you think it'll be in?"

"It better be." I hadn't really thought about the press. Of course all the New York papers will carry the story on the front page. Big John and all. But here in Pennsylvania so much depends on who publishes the local paper. "What paper do they get?" I ask Jim. "Is it put out by the monastery?"

"Monastery?" Jim looks at me.

"Yeah. Don't you live in a monastery or commune or something like that?"

Jim is dumbfounded. He looks at me to see if I'm putting him on and when he sees I'm serious he bursts out laughing as though he's losing his mind. I figure he's getting rid of some of the tension because I can't imagine what could be so hilarious. Finally he stops. "So you think we live in a monastery. Wow." He sits there smiling out the window as though I'm a real dummy.

"Hey, man, what's so funny?"

"Where'd you get this information, Eric?"

"What information?"

"Oh, this bit about monasteries."

He's starting to get on my nerves a little. "I don't know — some magazine or newspaper."

"And it said Mennonites live in monasteries?"

"Look, Jim. Mind setting me straight without making me feel like a fool?"

"Sorry. It struck me awful funny." Suddenly the smile is gone from his face and his eyes turn cold. "John is dead," he says, and there is nothing I can say. Death is so final. Life runs merrily along like a train turned loose upon an open track. And in the middle of the beginning we find the end. No more tracks. Only wind and cold sun and October.

"What if the church won't permit my folks to bury John?"

"You think they might put up a fight?"

"I don't know, Eric. I can't imagine what will happen. It's like John and I were foreigners at home these last years. I haven't been back since Christmas. And John — I doubt that the folks have seen him in two years. He said he'd never go home again."

"Big John said that?"

"Well, see, he and Pop had this big misunderstanding one time when we were home for vacation. John was sounding off and Pop told him he wasn't welcome there at home anymore. John said he didn't care — coming home was a pain anyhow. Pop got really mad. And John just up and left, the day before Christmas."

"What did your old man do?"

"Nothing. Mother worried a lot about John. See, before we went to school, John was like a favorite son around the place. But college changed that. To me he was basically the same old kid, even though I couldn't buy his radical politics. But Pop saw only the changes. He felt he had lost a son. I changed too, but not as much. I guess that's why they never threw me out. I wrote home pretty much too."

Evening has come to the country. It is sad and beautiful. The hostility of the day has softened in the light of twilight and as the train eases into the station I close my eyes and imagine I'm sitting in a hot steam bath. I haven't showered for days, what with the take-over and all. And now it's as though evening reaches out to wash our wounds and comfort us.

"Man, I forgot how beautiful it is," Jim says.

"Yeah, it's out of sight." I watch the mists come down from the hills and hover field to field like smoke across a plain as sunlight leaves the sky to campfires spread along the west.

It is dark when we step from the train. The station echoes with our walking and sends a dreary welcome to the few strangers who dare to stop here.

"Are they expecting us?" I ask Jim.

He stops and looks around. "They know we're coming. I told them I didn't know when the train would arrive."

"How far is it from here?"

"Our farm is six miles out of town. It's too far to walk. But maybe they're waiting outside." We walk down the narrow stairs and go out to the landing. Jim looks over the parking lot and shakes his head.

12

"Not here?"

"No, our car's not here," Jim says. His eyes run back across the lot again. "But wait. That looks like Eli's car." He runs and I run with him. A middle-aged man in farmer's clothes steps from the car. He and Jim embrace for a long time. They say nothing, searching each other's face.

"This is Eli, Eric," Jim says.

"Hi."

"Hello, Eric. It's nice you came." His hand is big and warm.

"Let's go home," Jim says.

Eli nods. "Yes, your parents will be waiting for you." He opens the door and helps me in. And even as I smell manure on his clothes, I wonder what is special about this man. He obviously has comforted Jim more in two minutes than I did the whole trip.

Once again I feel alone. Alone and afraid. I don't know why.

2

"Two or three eggs, Pop?" Jim's mother is asking from the big stove.

"One." Jim's dad is soft-spoken and small-featured, partly bald with hair thick around the back.

"What, only one? I'll make you two. How about you boys?" I've just had a whole education on cows, calves, and steers and breakfast is brewing in the big farm kitchen. It is seven o'clock and the milking is finished, the steers are fed, and the milk truck has come and gone. Wow. Generally I don't get up before ten in college, except for the crazy nine o'clock physics class.

"How many eggs, Eric?" Jim asks.

"Two."

"Two for each of us, Mom."

"Wilmer?"

"Well, Anna, I am pretty hungry this morning," Wilmer says.

"Three or four?"

"Four." Wilmer is the hired man.

"Okay, everyone gather round," Jim's dad says, sitting at the end of the table by the window. "Wilmer, get an extra chair."

They pray in silence. I look up to see what's

going on and Wilmer sits staring at me as though I'm spoiling his appetite. I glance at Jim but his eyes are closed and I get this feeling he might actually be praying. So I bow my head and wait for Mr. Witmer to say a quiet "Amen."

I knew nothing about Mennonites except the type of stuff one reads in the popular press. So I had a lot of misconceptions about what I might find at Jim and John's home. The Witmers are basically backwoods farmers, living a quiet provincial life, close to nature and far from the complexities of modern society. But I've really gotten turned on with the place in the few hours since we arrived last night. Of course, things are different than usual today, what with the funeral planning and all, but I told Jim during the milking that I envy him. "This is what the kids at school want," I said.

"Is it?" He didn't seem to agree.

"Sure, man, simplicity and all the fresh air in the world. And community. That's the big kick, Jim. Having a group of people to care about and to belong to."

"I suppose you're right," he said but I knew his mind was on other things.

After breakfast Mr. Witmer turns to Jim and says, "I'll give you a haircut before the uncles get here." I'm surprised. Jim wears his hair short like a law student — too short for me, in fact.

"Yeah, and trim those sideburns," Mrs. Witmer adds.

"Oh, Mom, take it easy."

"Don't argue with me, James Witmer." His mother

doesn't raise her voice, but the authority in it can't be mistaken. I see Wilmer staring at me and suddenly realize I guess I look pretty bad myself. I haven't had a cut in over a year. The last time I did, the stupid barber shaved my head as though he was some kind of crazy hair collector.

"I take it length of hair is part of your religion around here," I whisper to Wilmer. He doesn't answer as he sits there, still chewing on his four eggs and watching me as though I'm some strange animal.

The undertaker comes sometime before noon. Several relatives have arrived and they all go into the front room and close the door. Farmers in suspenders, bib overalls, and weathered faces, pink from shaving, troop into the white two-story house, shaking hands solemnly and looking very sober. They are followed by women in long dresses and wire-rimmed glasses, with white caps covering the backs of their heads, chatting quietly. Worried questions haunt their faces. These have come to bury Big John. The same Big John who was shouting at the cops only two days ago. Buried here in this lonely place. By people living in the seventeenth century. The place I've just fallen in love with suddenly seems strangely cold. It's October again and the Revolution is far away.

"I guess you can hang around with Wilmer." Jim is standing at my side.

"Yeah, sure." I try to act casual. "Hey, Jim, is everything okay? I mean, is there anything I can do?"

"No." He appears very calm. "Everything'll be okay. Look, Eric, this may take a while; so just hang loose. Okay? There's a lot of decisions to be made." For a moment I see panic deep in his eyes. He reaches out and takes my arm. "I don't suppose you are a praying man, kid, but if you are, I'd appreciate it."

"What is it, Jim?"

"I hope to God they don't send John to hell," he whispers. "It would be better if they hadn't all liked him so much." He looks toward the front room. "They're wonderful people, Eric. But they feel betrayed." He turns and follows his father in. They close the doors. And for the third time since I left the city I feel alone. Alone and afraid.

Wilmer and I meet Eli coming up the steps as we go out. Dressed in a worn suit and a big black hat, he carries several Bible-looking books.

"Good morning, Eric. Is Wilmer taking good care of you?"

"Yeah, he's okay."

"That's good." He puts his hand on my shoulder and his squeeze is gentle. His eyes are sad like water after a storm and his face bigger than a mountain, rugged with years of drought and floods.

"You're the prophet, aren't you?" I ask Eli.

"No." He smiles. "No, I'm just one of God's children."

But I know better. Later I discover he's the local minister. But it makes no difference. The moment I saw him at the station last night, I knew he was the prophet.

Wilmer leads me to the barn. I sit on a bale of hay while he fixes one of the pumps they use for

17

drawing water. The barn is quite modern.

"Why'd you ask him that?" Wilmer is lying on his back trying to turn a set screw.

"What?"

"I said why'd you say that to Eli?"

"Oh. I don't know, Wilmer. He just seems like a holy man."

"He is." Wilmer crawls out and wipes his hands. His big eyes watch me as though he expects me to disagree. I just chew a piece of hay. When he's cleaned his hands, he closes his toolbox and leans across the partition till his nose is less than ten inches from mine. "Eli's my best friend," he says. His breath stinks.

Wilmer invites me to walk along out to the mailbox. The day is chilly but the sky is clear with more blue than I've seen in months. I feel exhilarated like a child running free with the animals.

"I bet I can beat you out to the road," I say to Wilmer. He appears not to be very excited about the idea of a race. I decide to run anyhow. The air washes me. I close my eyes and laugh. My soul is clean and my heart less heavy.

"You like looking like a girl?" Wilmer says when he catches up with me.

"No," I shake my head. "No, I don't."

"Then why do you look like one?"

"Where I live I don't."

He opens the mailbox and pulls out two letters and a newspaper. He studies the letters. Then folding them into the paper, he starts for the house.

"Mind if I look at the paper?" I ask.

He takes the letters, puts them in his coat, and hands me the paper. But before I can take it, he pulls it back. There in bold headlines across the front page marches the news: "Local Hippie Killed in New York Riot." Wow. There's a picture of Big John, so square I hardly recognize him. Must be his high school picture. At least they didn't get hold of any of those national wire service photos.

Wilmer goes to pieces before my eyes as he reads it. His eyes bulge in his face and his breathing chokes. He begins to shake all over. I can't tell if he's angry or afraid. He stands there like a human sundial, the paper clutched in his hands, trembling in the bright autumn sun. And the time of day I see in Wilmer's shadow is late. Too late, perhaps.

The newspaper turns out to be one of these local strait-laced chronicles that labels everything that moves. "John Witmer, son of Mr. and Mrs. Menno Witmer, was killed in a student rebellion at the university early yesterday. Officials stated that the students were armed and burning buildings in this communist-inspired riot that took the lives of two other students and one policeman. Police said they had arrested twenty-four students and two professors."

There is more. But I don't care to see it. I tear the paper from Wilmer's hands and rip it to pieces. I run up the hill to a cornfield and throw the pieces among the stalks. Wilmer is still standing in the center of the road when I get back.

I would have sworn until now that I would never be able to sympathize with people who oppose

19

the Revolution. But here stands a man ten years my superior, a peasant in smelly farmer's clothes who would have never known the truth if the newspaper had not come today. Death he can cope with. Even though he's disappointed that John died out there in the big evil city. But the news of Big John's politics paralyzes Wilmer. It cuts his world wide open and he is helpless.

It touches something deep in me I forgot was there. I turn toward the wind and weep.

When we get back to the house, we sit on the western side of the old garage and listen to the song of the wind through the wood. There is a wailing in the song, but it is a soft kind of wailing. I suppose on the east side it might be less soothing.

At first I sit beside Wilmer but he moves away from me. So we sit, several yards apart, silent. Noon passes and the sun falls toward the hills. There is nothing to do.

Jim wakens me. I must have fallen asleep. Wilmer's gone and the shadows are long. My stomach aches for food.

"Sorry, man," Jim says. "I never thought it would take this long. We had almost everything settled by one o'clock. Then Uncle Rufus arrived in his big shiny car and his big flashy clothes. He's one of these people who thinks spending a lot of money and dressing loud is the same as being liberal. It was a bad scene, Eric."

"One o'clock? He'd probably seen the newspaper."

"Oh, sure. Well, he has television and everything. He actually saw John on one of the news reels. Boy, was he mad. Destroying property is more of a sin than destroying life to Uncle Rufus. He just blurted it all out. I could have died. We had just reached an agreement on how to conduct the service. Eli would preach and the general tone was to be cool but not totally condemning. And the funeral would be held in the church. It was turning out better than I expected. Until Rufus came. Now there's to be no service in the church. A short ceremony at the grave is more than he deserves, says Rufus."

Jim and I walk toward the house. Wilmer is shouting at some steers in the barnyard and the dog is barking. Most of the relatives are gone and the big porch hangs like a shadow on the faded face of the farmhouse.

"I guess in the end," Jim says, "one belongs to the people who bury him." He looks off toward the hills behind the house. "There's a little graveyard up there. Tomorrow we dig a grave for John."

Maybe it sounds romantic, but it isn't. It's too cruel. Big John died with most of his life still in him. Died for a cause these people cannot understand. But they are the ones who bury him. I guess those who live longest have the last word.

"At least they didn't bury him some other place like Uncle Rufus suggested. Mother wouldn't hear of it."

We meet the undertaker on the porch. He looks as though he should be taken under himself. His voice is high and fragile as he speaks to Jim. "I'll fix him up so he'll look like he used to. That's difficult — but it's possible."

"Fine." Jim shows nothing in his face. "Thanks for being patient."

"Oh, that's okay," the undertaker says. He talks like a man grown weary of his job with more work than he can handle. "Pardon my saying it," he says, "the dead must be respected, of course, but it always takes people so long to decide what to do with them."

"You're wrong," Jim tells the old man. "The dead teach us how to live. It's memories from the past that help us find the way."

"But we all must die someday, young man."

"True."

The undertaker grins and walks away. His step is weary. Weary with years and too much death.

A jeep comes driving up as the undertaker is leaving. The two men in the jeep talk a bit with the undertaker and keep looking up at us.

"I wonder who they are," Jim says.

"Their hair's too long for around here," I tell him. "I don't think I like what I see."

The two men are getting out. Both carry cameras. I start down the steps. "You stay here, Jim. I'll check them out."

The big man in the red jacket is already snapping. The other guy is pulling a television camera out of the back seat.

"Hold it right there," I say. "One more snap of that shutter and you'll have no camera."

The big red jacket comes walking toward me. Click. Clickety-click-click. I wait until he's close enough. Then I smile and kick him in the stomach. Hard. I

22

catch the camera as he buckles up, his hands holding his big red front. I tear the camera open and expose the film.

"This is private property, Red Jacket," I say in a real low voice I use for scaring people. "I see you here again and we'll hold a funeral for you. Now beat it."

Back on the porch, Jim asks me who they were.

"Oh, some amateur television people from the city. They won't be back. Not today, at least."

But tomorrow is another day.

3

Today they bury Big John. In a small family graveyard high among the trees on the slope behind the house his grandfather built. Mennonite soil, Jim called it yesterday when we were digging the grave. Virgin forest, settled by Mennonite peasants, fresh from Europe. Two hundred and fifty years ago.

That's one thing about the Mennonites. History. They're married to history. They remind me of the Jews I know. In this little family cemetery here on the hill, Jim showed me markers for all his ancestors down through the years. He is the tenth generation since his family arrived in America.

I sit on the rail fence, waiting. They should be arriving shortly. They're coming from the funeral home in town. Big John on his last trip.

The sky is masked with that cheerlessness characteristic of cloudy days thinking of winter. Nature stands aloof and expressionless as another Witmer is laid to rest.

The twins have a brother, I discovered yesterday when we were preparing the grave. Or rather, they had a brother. He died in a tractor accident four years ago. Simon was his name. Jim smiled as he told me about it. He asked if I'd ever heard of Peter, James, and John before.

I see them coming in the lane now. There must be thirty cars in the procession. The funeral is certainly not that of a hero, but Jim says all the relatives will probably show up anyhow. "Funerals are big things with our people," he said.

Poor Jim. He's lost his best friend, his own twin and brother. But he's had no time for grief. Between planning funeral details, refusing to speak to the press, and trying to explain John's death to hostile relatives, he's been digging a grave and consoling his parents. I try to help. But most of the time there is nothing I can do.

It didn't take long to see the relatives didn't like me around. That's why I stayed away from the viewing last night. No point in making things worse. The Revolution will hardly take hold among these folks anyhow.

I climb down and step into the woods, watching the people come up the hill in their black cars. One family in a horse and buggy came early and parked by the barn. Now as I watch the buggy follow the cars up the hill like a black, horse-drawn carriage of death, I shudder deep in my soul and turn away. It must be a dream, this scene. A bad dream. How can these austere people bury Big John like a prodigal son? But what can I do? I thought maybe some other kids from the university would try to come for the funeral, but none showed up. The riots are getting worse every day, from what I hear on Jim's radio. So I must bury Big John alone. Alone with these people.

I stand in the trees, watching helplessly. They sing the funeral hymns in a slow staccato chant that hangs like sorrow and condemnation in the tiny cemetery, waiting for the wind to come and sweep it far away, beyond the indifferent skies to a heaven where all is well. But there is no wind.

An old man steps forward and reads some pieces from the Bible. And then he prays. His hands are gnarled from years of work and his voice shakes with his words. He prays for forgiveness and peace. And he gives thanks. Once again I am touched.

I keep being torn between loving these people and hating them. They seem so crude and quick to condemn. They purposely keep their children from learning about the rest of the world. It's as though they think they have a corner on truth. And yet some of them obviously know more about life and living than I do. And so I despise their dogmatism and admire their simplicity.

Eli steps to the graveside, his Bible open and his eyes toward heaven. His forehead is lined with sorrow and his eyes are filled with tears that spill over and run slowly down his cheeks. He drops his eyes to the people and he looks at them, standing there in the cold October afternoon. For a long moment he doesn't speak. It's as though he's pleading with them to open their hearts. He looks at the casket and bows his head. His voice is steady and relaxed, so soft I can hardly hear it.

"God is here," he says. "God is not out there someplace, beyond those sullen clouds, far from our grief and confusion. God is here among us. And where

God is, there is light and there is love."

The people are listening to Eli. Like poetry on the lips of a prophet, his words reach out and touch his little congregation.

"Eight years ago when I first came to Pennsylvania," Eli goes on, "I remember visiting in Menno Witmer's home. His wife introduced their three sons — Peter, James, and John. And I soon found out they were delightful boys. I confess sometimes I almost wished they were mine." He looks at Jim's parents as he talks.

"Four summers ago we buried Simon. It was hot here on the hill as James and John laid their young brother to rest. We prayed and wept and tried to understand.

"Today we bury John. And it it is cold here on the hill. Things are very different. Most of us have neither prayed nor wept, Nor have we tried to understand. John was a favorite with many of us, full of life and full of fun. He cared about us and we cared about him." Eli pauses thoughtfully. His eyes pass over the black bonnets and black hats, peering into their faces. For a moment he hesitates on Rufus with his new green coat, standing beside his short wife, bedecked in red coat, red jewelry, and red lips. A lot of red and a dab of green in a sea of black.

"If we were honest, we would admit that we are not so pure ourselves. I'm not here to condone everything John did in his years of college. I'm not here to condemn John, either. For one thing, I don't really know the whole story. John was concerned, that I know. He always was that way. And for that I'll always remember him."

Eli begins to pace a bit. "Why did God allow John to die now, when he was a troubled, angry young man? Why couldn't John come home to us and live like the rest? Was John ready?"

Eli's eyes dry. "Those are hard questions. But more important is another question: Were we ready? Were we ready, brothers and sisters?"

I hear nothing more of what the prophet says. A breeze has begun to sweep through the trees and I shiver. They sing a final song and lower the casket into the ground. And as the long black coats turn to go back to their black cars and ride off into the ashen horizon, it begins to rain.

I hear a click behind me. Red Jacket looks up from his camera and smiles. I look away. What's the use? It's all over now. Big John is asleep with his ancestors, lying in a fresh grave beside one brother and waiting for the other.

I pull my guitar from its hiding place in the leaves and walk out of the trees. Eli is talking with Rufus and Mrs. Rufus. Jim is helping the young cousin pallbearers shovel. The parents are still standing at the same spot, watching silently.

"But you know the Bible says that those who don't confess the Son cannot be saved," Rufus is saying to Eli. "And I'm not talking about dressing plain, and all that. You know I'm one of the most liberal Mennonites around. I'm talking about personal salvation."

"Brother Rufus, I know you are concerned — "

"Concerned! Eli, I'm talking about truth. Why,

John didn't even believe in the new birth." Rufus emphasizes each word with a jabbing forefinger.

"Brother Rufus, this is not the place or the time," Eli stands his ground.

Rufus takes his wife's arm and starts toward their car. He stops abruptly and comes back to Eli. "You disappoint me," he whispers hoarsely; "you had a chance to speak out and you were scared." And with that accusation, the new green coat turns and leaves the little graveyard.

Eli sees that I have heard. His eyes are sad and troubled. He sighs as he watches Rufus ride down the hill in his chariot of truth. "I'm sorry," the prophet says. "God was here and Rufus missed Him."

The pallbearers are gone and Jim is helping his parents into the old battered car. It's a late fifty model and one of its back tires is a faded whitewall spare. The rain splotches dusty patterns on the hood.

A young woman is talking to Jim's mother as we come walking up. Her dress is a bit shorter than the older women's and her bonnet is much smaller. As she turns to us, Eli puts his arm around her and kisses her cheek. Her face is much younger than I thought.

"Eric, I don't suppose you've met my daughter, Hazel," Eli says.

"No, I haven't," I say. "I didn't know you had a family."

Eli smiles. "Twelve children, Eric."

"Twelve?"

"Yes, eight girls and four boys. Hazel is the oldest."

"Glad to meet you, Hazel," I say, looking into her dark eyes. She's beautiful in an austere Mennonite sort of way. She looks at me without a smile.

The rain falls faster now. "You going down to the house?" I ask Jim.

"No," he says. "Not yet." We start across the open field, the rain in our faces. "I want to think," Jim says.

Hazel comes running after us. Jim turns and goes back to her. They stand talking as the others wait in the car. Dusk creeps in across the valley far below. The rain is cold.

When Jim and I are all alone we walk to the edge of the woods, behind the broken rail fence of the graveyard, and I sing some of Big John's favorite rock pieces. It's as though we're giving him a proper funeral, now that the others are gone. I play them over and over, dancing tiny steps in the wet fallen leaves and strumming more soul out of my strings than they've ever sung before. The wind is stronger now and the rain falls gently on the fresh grave.

Our little dance is like a celebration. A celebration of life — in time of death. Something Big John would understand.

It's getting dark. Like a curtain of ever-darkening smoke, the late afternoon is driven toward the west. And Jim and I sit in the rain, pulling our coats about our shoulders. We sing a hymn that no one else can understand. It's like two strangers meeting in the evening, talking, touching, and experiencing what no one else will ever know. Only it's two very different worlds that have met here in this graveyard tonight. And so we sing a hymn together, a hymn no man can ever write or sing again. It's our way of burying Big John.

"You feel it when you lose a twin," Jim says. "I lost a part of me when Simon died. But not as much. I guess I'm older now. And John and I were so close."

He walks toward the graves. "We used to be happy, Eric," he says. "The three of us were in love with life, hardworking and innocent and just as happy as the grass was green." But today the grass is brown with death as Jim walks among the graves, a lonely figure in the closing night, standing on the ground that will someday open to receive his own body.

Jim lifts his head toward the heavens and a great burst of anguish pours from his lips and mingles with the sound of wind and rain. At last Jim is alone and he weeps like a frightened child. I slip away through the woods and listen to the night. If there is a God, I'm sure he'll hear Jim tonight.

I start for the buildings. The rain has matted my hair to my head and it is washing my spinal cord clean, running on down my legs and into my shoes.

At the barn I find Wilmer finishing the milking by himself. I take off my coat and help him carry the hay. He doesn't even look at me as we work. The sound of cows munching, the sound of the milker, and the sound of rain. That is all. That and the smell of cows. I've almost learned to like it by now.

As we snap the yard light on and head for the house, I see Jim standing in the rain below the barn, looking down across the meadow to the stream. His eyes are red and heavy as he stares into the night.

"Hazel used to date my brother," Jim says.

"You mean Eli's daughter?"

He nods. "She always came on a little too strong for me. But John liked her a lot."

"Recently?"

"Before we went to college." Jim turns toward the house. "It looks like she and Eli are still here. Probably stayed for supper." He turns back to the shadows. "She asked me if John had to die, Eric. 'Did John really have to die?' That's how she said it. She wasn't mad; she wasn't hostile. She simply asked."

"Did you try to answer her?"

Jim glances toward the house again. The water is running down his face and he looks like an old man in the half-light.

"Tomorrow I take the first train back to the city," he says.

"But tomorrow is Saturday. Why not wait until Sunday?"

He looks at me and shakes his head. "You're some friend," he says with a faint smile. We walk to the house and enter by the side door. He pauses to take off his coat and shake the rain from his head.

"I told her it looked that way to me."

"What?"

"You asked about Hazel," he says. "I didn't know what to say. So I told her John was all caught up in trying to change the world. And that's risky."

We go in and sneak up to Jim's room to change clothes. It's a big room with a high ceiling. Big enough for three.

We hear them talking in the kitchen. "We better go down," Jim says after we've changed into something dry and warm.

"Okay. I'm hungry, anyhow."

He smiles. "Me too."

Wilmer is eating by himself at the table. Eli and Jim's father sit in a corner talking quietly. The women are washing the dishes.

"Got any to spare there, Wilmo?" Jim says, taking a potato slice from the hired man's plate.

"Wilmo?" I ask.

"Yeah, Wilmo. That's what we always called you, isn't that right, Mr. Big Eater?" Jim smiles, taking another slice. Wilmer stares at him, his mouth moving faster in an effort to make more room for the food in question. "Get your own," he says.

Hazel brings us each a plate of food, humming softly to herself.

"You really a hippie?" she says, looking at me with those dark eyes. Wow. I keep forgetting how different I must look.

"No," I say without batting an eye. "No, I'm the all American boy." Jim laughs.

"You don't have to try to act smart," she snaps back. "I ask a straight question; I want a straight answer."

She goes back to helping Mrs. Witmer. "Don't mind her," Jim says. "She can turn the kindness on as fast as she turns it off."

"Really?" I wonder what he means. And even as I wonder, I realize I'm not ready to leave for the city quite yet. There is a prophet here I've been wanting to learn more about. And now I find he has a daughter. That makes two to learn about.

4

"I never liked high places," I tell Jim, who has postponed his return to the city. "I'd rather stay here on the ground if they can use me." It is Monday morning and we have joined the neighbors in a barn raising for John Zook. The ruins have been cleaned away and a new building begins to rise out of the ashes.

"You have a hammer, young fella?" A bearded man is asking me.

"Yeah, right here."

"Follow me. We can use you over here." He leads me to a group of men who are assembling one section of the wall. "You ever hammered before?" he asks, handing me some nails.

"Yeah — a good bit. I built sets for plays in college."

"Plays, huh?" I can't tell if he likes that or not. "May I ask your name?"

"Sure," he smiles; "sure, go ahead."

"You don't want to tell me?"

"It makes no difference to me." He hammers a nail into the joint with three strong strokes, chewing casually the whole time. He spits tobacco juice.

"So what is your name?" I ask.

"Bart Beiler," he says, never giving his chew a rest.

"Bart? I never heard of that before. Is that a nickname you picked up someplace?"

"Nickname?" He looks at me. "That ain't no nickname. Bart — it's short for Bartholomew."

"Oh, I see. Bartholomew, of course. Sorry." We hammer for a while and I'm painfully aware that he averages five nails for every three I manage to hammer into the stubborn wood. The cold weather is hard on the hands.

"Your name?" His beard turns in my direction.

"What? Oh, mine. Eric."

"Eric? That a nickname?" Bart's smile lights up his eyes.

"No." I decide to laugh since the joke's on me. "No, just Eric."

"Last name?"

I look at him solemnly. "Just Eric." He smiles, and I think I've made a friend.

The sun keeps us warm as we work. Dozens of men hammer, climb, lift, call, and laugh, and every few minutes a new section of the big barn is moved into place and nailed. A clean wood skeleton against the sky. Impressive. Mr. Zook's barn burns in a thunderstorm and early one frosty morning a few weeks later the neighbors come and build him another barn. It's hard to believe.

"You a Mennonite?" I ask Bart.

"Me? Oh, no. I'm Amish."

"Amish?" I can't keep the curiosity from my voice. I

should have known. I'd always heard there were lots of Amish here in Pennsylvania. "What's the difference?" I ask him.

"What?" Bart stands up and leans toward me, his hand cupped over his ear as he tries to hear above the hammering.

"What's the difference between the Mennonites and Amish?" I shout.

"It's very simple," I hear a female voice behind me answer. I turn and see Hazel smiling innocently. "I'm Mennonite," she says, "and Bart's Amish."

"I didn't know you were here, Hazel."

She laughs. "I like to surprise people." Her eyes laugh, too, half hidden under dark hair and bright scarf. She offers me a cup. "Hot chocolate?"

"I'd be delighted."

She pours as one accomplished in pouring.

I hand the first cup to Bart. He drinks noisily. "That's right good, Hazel," he says.

"Thank you, Bart. Your wife made it."

"Lydia did, did she? I better have a second cup," he winks.

The chocolate is hot and warms me the whole way down. Hazel watches me drink. "It's good," I tell her.

"I didn't think you'd know how to use that hammer," she says.

"Oh, I'm not as good as Bart, but I do okay."

"Your father here, Hazel?" Bart asks, wiping some chocolate from his beard.

"No. He had to go to the hospital. Maybe he'll be around later." She looks at me. "I think he wants to talk with you."

"Who? Me?"

She nods, her cheeks alive with color in the cold day as she takes her kettle and starts toward another group of men. I start after her, reaching out to stop her.

"What's your father want with me?"

"You scared?"

"Scared? No, why'd you say that?"

"You sound scared." She laughs. Whatever Jim said about her being able to turn on as fast as she turns off must be true. "Father wants you to come for supper tonight."

"Really?"

She nods. "You going to be there?" I ask. She nods a second time. And her eyes are laughing once again as she turns and walks away.

Wow. The prophet invites the hippie to dinner? Sounds a wee bit far out. Especially when Hazel has as mysterious a grip on life as her father seems to have on God.

Hot lunch is served for all the volunteers in the corn shed. The women rush around, talking, laughing, and making sure the men get plenty to eat. The soup is rich, the sandwiches thick with ham and chicken and bologna. Bart dips his sandwiches in the soup and sort of sucks them into his mouth. The whole scene reminds me of a festival. A festival of volunteer workers. The afternoon hurries past as we put the finishing touches on the big building. And when the farmers leave to do their chores, a new barn stands like a shelter in the closing gray.

At six-thirty I find myself alone, seated at the end

of a table full of hungry children as Eli prays his thanks. The children join in the "Amen." Hazel and her sisters serve the food. I wonder where their mother is.

The boys look like little prophets sitting silent and obedient on their backless bench against the wall. They scoop large portions from the heaping dishes and stuff their mouths to overflowing.

"How did you like the barn raising, Eric?" Eli asks.

"I was impressed, Eli. Does it often happen?"

"Well, yes, pretty often. Whenever a barn burns."

"Is it true Mr. Zook won't put any lightning rods on his barn?" I ask. One of the men had told me that.

"Oh, John will. He probably won't take out insurance but he'll put up some rods."

"No insurance?"

Eli smiles. "I guess that's hard to understand. Some of our people believe the Bible teaches us to trust the Lord in some of these matters. I don't personally see it as being a matter of trusting the Lord. I understand it as brotherhood. That's why we formed our own insurance company — to take care of each other."

The kitchen is a humble one. Small, with worn furniture, bare painted walls, decorated with calendars and little religious mottoes. The aroma of home-grown food, the murmur of children and clinking of plates. A home.

When I first met Eli I thought him a traveler, a lonely man who was misunderstood because he spoke from the depths of his being. But now I see him as a father to twelve growing children, who eat at his table and listen to his prayers.

"How long have you lived here?" I ask.

"Only three years, Eric," he says. "We moved here after Miriam died." The children, suddenly quiet, look at their father as he eats. "Miriam was my wife," he says.

"Oh, I see. I'm sorry."

"We loved her while she could be with us, Eric. And when the Lord took her, we thanked Him for letting us have her as long as He did." The prophet's eyes move around the table, reassuring each of the children as they watch and listen. "The Lord has been good to us," he says.

For a moment a part of me deep inside wants to cry. There's something of paradise here in this room. Secondhand clothing, backless benches, and no mother. And yet these children are some of the happiest in the world. They are loved by a man who teaches them that God loves them too. It's like a little miracle.

Hazel is watching me from her work by the stove. The pale kitchen light falls on her like a soft gown. As beautiful as the children, an angel for the prophet. Possessed with the fire of living. Her laughing eyes are serious now, serious and full of music. Like the singing and serious promises of dawn after a dark and troubled night. For Hazel is more than an angel. She is a mother to the other eleven.

"Would you like to be one of us?" she asks me after the meal.

I'm not sure what she means. But something

passes between us in the silence, and it doesn't matter what she means.

Eli and I sit by the stove and talk. Hazel and her sisters clean the dishes while the older boys go to the barn to finish a few chores. Eli watches each child with interest.

"Do you come from a large family, Eric?"

"Me? No. I'm the only child." No point in his knowing all the details about my never seeing my father, or my mother's doing her share of shopping around. It all seems so foreign here in this little kitchen.

"And what does your father do for a living?" He rocks in his chair, eyes watching me.

"Oh, my life was not really that interesting," I tell him. "It was so different from things around here."

"Yes, of course. I'm sorry if I sound over-interested."

"No, no, not at all."

He rocks again. "What are you preparing for in college, Eric? Do you want to teach?"

"I don't know. I'm in English but I've been interested in politics. Or rather, I should say I was interested in politics. Before Big John got clubbed. Now I don't know."

"I guess things have quieted down at the university."

"Yes, the national guard was sent in over the weekend. When Jim decided to stay here for a few days longer, I called some of my friends and they said things were pretty bad. The fighting had stopped

41

and the police were making a lot of arrests."

"May I ask you a rather straight question, Eric?"

"Sure." I still don't know why he invited me to supper. Perhaps there's something he wants to say.

"Why do the students burn buildings and riot like they do? We hear all kinds of things out here in the country. But what are the real reasons, Eric?"

I look at him as he rocks and wonder how one begins to explain. None of us ever ask why anymore. It's too late, perhaps — too late to ask why.

"That's hard to answer, Eli. It's like there's something very human deep inside us that comes bursting forth, crying out against the killing and the selfishness and the hypocrisy."

"But if you hate violence, why do you use violence yourselves?"

I watch a tiny bug go speeding along the floor and underneath a rug. "I guess because the only things that ever change are brought about by violence," I say.

He is silent. I can hear him breathing as he watches his daughters at the sink. He's thinking it over. Finally he begins to rock again.

"Could it be that they need God, Eric?" His eyes meet mine.

Wow! My first impulse is to laugh. God! God is the trouble with this country. Everyone destroying everyone else in the name of religion. Protecting property and injustice and a particular style of life by quoting the Bible. The town where I grew up was full of it.

"They don't need God, Eli," I say. "He's had his

chance." I see a quiver of sadness flow across his face like wind through the trees on the face of a great mountain.

"But are they truly forgiven?" he says, his voice low and intense.

"Forgiven?"

"Eric, God loves all of us and wants us to be His children. Through Jesus we find the forgiveness that makes us His. But that means forsaking all to follow Him." He states it gently, simply, as though it needs no defense. And then he closes his eyes and rocks back and forth. There's nothing for me to say.

Hazel brings us hot chocolate and cookies. "Are you ready for family worship, Papa?" she asks her father.

"Yes, as soon as the children gather," Eli says. And as each of the older children brings a Bible and takes his place with the younger ones at the table, Eli takes his Bible and hymnal from the shelf. I sit at the end of the table and listen. Hazel leads them in singing an old hymn I faintly remember from many years ago. Everyone helps. There is happiness in their song. Happiness and home. The simple beauty of this humble kitchen, far from perfect, but so unlike anything I've ever known. A children's choir and their father. Singing a hymn of love and peace.

Eli reads about Nicodemus. He looks at each of the children as he reads. And then he prays. I don't hear much of it until the end. "Bless Eric, dear Lord," he is saying, "and show him Your love. May he find You and love You. We thank You for his friendship. Keep us, dear Lord, and may our lives be joyful sacrifices in Your praise."

When the prayer is ended, the children start for bed. And after they're all gone I sit with Eli, alone at the table, still stunned by his prayer. Man, I never heard anyone mention my name in prayer before. And if someone had, I'm sure I would have laughed. But not at Eli's table. He prays and God hears.

"Well, Eric, thanks for visiting us tonight," he says. "As you can see, our place is nothing special but I trust that doesn't matter. We have more than we need, really. The Lord has been good." The smile engraved across his face is satisfied and wise.

I get up to go. He brings my coat and shakes my hand. "God loves you, Eric," he says. "Don't settle for anything less."

All the way back to Jim's place I hear those children singing as their father prays. And something deep in me is frightened by it all. "Don't settle for anything less," he said. Less than what?

Jim is reading in his room. "Nice evening?" he asks.

"I don't know, Jim. It was all so strange. That man has got something I don't. But what is it?"

"I think it's God," Jim says, as he crawls into bed.

He snaps the light off and I'm alone in the dark. The blankets are warm and the night wind's a song. But I cannot sleep.

5

At the foot of the big farm bed, the window lights up and darkens and lights up again as night clouds hurry past the moon on some exciting, nocturnal chores and throw their moving silhouettes across the pane. In the half-light, I watch Jim's boyish face, relaxed in sleep, gently rise and fall with his steady breathing. The last of the Witmer boys, asleep but very much alive.

I wonder whether years ago the three of them might not have slept together in one of these gigantic beds on some of the cold winter nights. It must have been a sight to behold. I guess Jim's mother would have lots of stories to tell. But most mothers don't tell. Like the silhouettes who dance across that windowpane and hurry off before their secrets are discovered.

Often when I'm awake at night I can feel my heart beating in my big toe. And it's not all in my head, either. Man, it really throbs away, so hard I'm scared it might awaken Jim. So I roll over on my side and watch the shadows on the wall.

Sleepless nights are not all that uncommon to me. They're even sort of fun sometimes. I always hear the wildest things at night.

But tonight is not an ordinary night. As Jim's breathing harmonizes with the wind around the corner of the old house, I hear the sound of children singing. The hymn they sing and the prayer their father prays have gripped me with a mysterious hypnotism I've never felt before. My heart beats faster and I breathe deep as I lie in the big bed, watching the wall. I try to reason with myself, but the singing will not stop. It's as though someone is calling me and I'm trying to decide to answer back.

Time passes rapidly. I try to understand why my whole being is recoiling in a desperate attempt to hold back. Hold back from what, I do not know. But it's all tied up in Eli's prayer and the sound of his children singing. And I keep holding back.

The singing is so loud now that I can hear each individual voice. It's like some far out trip. Except it's just as real as my breathing. It's not a dream. Something has taken hold of me and will not let me go.

I slip out of bed and into cold trousers and shoes. I take my shirt and move toward the stairs, carefully avoiding the bed. Wham. I bump into a chair and the noise makes me jump. I freeze and wait for Jim to sit up and ask me what in the world I'm trying to do. But his boyish face doesn't stir.

Downstairs the shadows race across the big farm kitchen like envoys from one corner of the earth to another. I slip out the side door. The wind comes rushing across the porch and breathes ice against my skin. My teeth chatter and my eyes fight off the cold. But even now I hear the singing and the prayer.

The stables are not as cold. I stand listening to the dark beasts fill the barn with their slumber. The world has gone to bed and everyone's asleep. Everyone except me and the clouds.

Again I try to reason with myself. The talk about God can't be shaking me up this much, can it? No, of course not. But this is more than talk tonight. Eli is more than talk. Eli is possessed by this living presence that calls me tonight. And I can't block it out of my mind. It's larger than my mind. It's all about me, not so much following me as going on ahead. Very strange. Strange and mysterious. And real.

The moonlight down across the meadow transforms the landscape into a frozen dreamland of dirty white. Impersonal and lifeless, almost indifferent. Everything is frozen or asleep it seems. Everything but the voices of those children.

The car starts without trouble. I wait until I'm nearly on the road before I turn on the headlights. The plastic seat covers are just as cold as the steering wheel and I pull my collar tight around my neck.

The road is empty all the way to Eli's place. And the closer I get, the louder the singing. My mind reaches out to grasp it all. I try to understand the empty fear in which the singing echoes deep inside me. The fear is familiar but the echo is new.

Even in the moonlight, when things have that dreamy, romantic extra touch, Eli's place does not. It has the fallen-togetherness of a poor farmer's place. The equipment around the back, the little sheds built against other built-on sheds, the broken fence around the yard. And there is no dog to awaken.

I stand before the door, shivering and scared. Why am I here? What is this stupid fear within me, driving me to such strange action? What is the voice that calls? I stare at myself in the glass of the door and once again try to cope with it all. But it is bigger than I am, bigger than life.

I knock softly. What if the twelve should awaken and come crying, in fear of this long-haired kid who stands at their door in the middle of this frozen night? This night, washed in light, as bright as the morning. What if Eli is not the prophet he seems? How can I know that the roar in my soul can be quieted by the words of this man?

Suddenly the singing stops. The roar stands still in my ears as I wait by the door. I knock again, harder this time. The roar is gone but the voice that calls me is clearer than ever. And I shiver in the silent wind of its tones.

I try the doorknob to see if it's locked. It is not. The warmth of the house comes sweeping out to carry me in as I close the door behind me. A light is shining in the hall and I move toward the stairs. "O God, what am I doing in this stranger's house?"

The bathroom's at the top of the stairs. I used it last night. So Eli's room must be the one with the big door just across.

I freeze in my tracks as I come to my senses. What am I doing, prowling around this house like a killer? What do I want? "O God," I breathe through my teeth, "God, what do I want?"

But I cannot turn back. There is something within me that tells me to follow. And with all my heart I want to follow. Part fear and part hope.

When I reach the top of the stairs, I see that all of the doors along the hall are standing ajar. And the sound of sleeping comes from each door.

I tiptoe to the first, hoping to find Eli. But I see four little faces all in a row in two small beds, side by side. Four little prophetesses, no doubt.

The next room's a bit larger and the beds are facing the opposite way. In the mirror on the wall I see four more heads. But the room is full of bicycle wheels, small pieces of log, and little heaps of clothes. It must be the boys.

I glance across the hall, through the smallest doorway of all, and I see a beautiful woman, asleep by herself, dark hair falling about her cheeks. The moonlight on her forehead and the smile on her lips belong to a child. But the face is a woman's. Hazel asleep.

I stand in the doorway watching her. And the pounding in my heart has so barely changed its tone, I hardly know the difference. But the voice going on ahead, calling and urging me, is still there. The beauty of this woman is not the beauty of her father. But they are very much alike.

Suddenly she is asleep no more. Her eyelids open and she is looking at me in the darkness. She jerks upward in her bed. A startled cry escapes her lips. But no one hears.

Man, am I scared! All of a sudden I want to run. But her eyes hold me there in the doorway.

"What are you doing here?" Her voice is colder than the night.

"I'm sorry, Hazel. I've got to see your father."

"What for?" Her eyes are daring me to tell the truth.

I don't know what to say. The voice inside and outside, all around me calling. And the fear that keeps holding back.

"I'm scared," I say, stepping into her room.

For a long moment she looks at me. "Come here," she says.

I watch her closely as I move toward her bed. With her hair hanging loose, she is more beautiful than ever. But her eyes command me to beware.

"You came back to steal, didn't you?" she asks.

"No." I don't know how to explain.

"Maybe you think we're easy to take advantage of around here," her whisper intensifies, "but we're not. Now just explain what you're doing here, Eric."

"Hazel, I'm truly sorry. But I had to come. I have to see your father."

"Why?"

"I swear I can't explain. I just can't sleep. A voice keeps calling me and I can't make it stop. Man, it's really strange."

Her face looks up at mine and her eyes are friendly now. She slips out of bed and takes my arm. "Here, sit down while I get Papa." Her touch warms me.

Long moments later she returns. "He said he'll be downstairs in a minute or two. Come, I'll make some coffee." She puts her arm around me as we head down the stairs. And in the warmth there is something kind and understanding.

In the kitchen she works noiselessly while Eli and I sit by the stove. None of us speak for a long time. She brings the coffee and goes back upstairs, leaving me alone with her father. And the clock in the hall chimes twice.

"Look, Eli, I'm sorry about this," I start in.

"Never mind," he says, laying a hand on my arm. "I'm happy you felt free to come."

He waits for me to go on, and I think that's why I go on. This man has learned to wait. He does not pressure or scorn me or push me aside. He waits. And in waiting there is caring.

I tell him all about my cold, sleepless night, the voices, the singing, the prayer. He sips as he listens, only occasionally asking a question or saying, "Oh, yes" or "I'm glad" or "God knows." And when the clock in the hall strikes three, I am still telling him my story. The story of my life, it turns out.

Then suddenly, out of the pieces of story and the fragments of conversation, Eli touches the heart of it all. "I believe God is calling you," he says. And something deep down in me answers yes. I can't explain what happens to me when all of a sudden I let go. The roar goes away and there is singing again. Only singing that's with, not against. There's a warm spirit sweeping my soul and the joy that is washing me clean makes me cry. And Eli and I talk on and on, till the morning within me is brighter than the moonlight outside. And the strangeness is real and the joy is complete. The words that we speak are happiness and worship.

The prophet and I kneel in the dawn and I pour

out my heart in a prayer of my own, confessing that Jesus has saved, the Spirit has washed, and that God in His love has forgiven and healed. And the healing is real.

The clock chimes again, and this time it is five. We rise from our knees and embrace like long lost brothers discovering each other at dawn. And the light of the new day is a joy.

I slip back to Jim's place and park the car. The barn is stirring and the chickens are calling. But the big house is still wrapped in sleep.

I reach the bedroom without a noise. Jim hasn't moved since I left. I take off my clothes and get into bed, pulling the covers close to my shoulders. And as I close my eyes to catch my first happy sleep, an alarm clock starts ringing in another part of the house.

The next thing I hear is the sound of a gun. My watch tells me it's past noon as I leap out of bed. I run to the window and see Wilmo shooting pigeons off the roof of the silo.

Jim's mother has food waiting for me. "Wilmer's getting ready for hunting season," she says. "He never gets anything but he sure shoots a lot."

"When does the season begin?" I ask.

"On Saturday. Menno never was much of a hunter himself. But the boys used to go all the time when they lived at home. John was the best, I guess. He and James always came back with a rabbit or a pheasant. But Wilmer never got a thing."

"I never went hunting myself," I say. And suddenly the world is much the same again. Last night seems like a dream. But I feel a sense of happiness and

52

freedom deep inside. What it all means and how it changes things I can't be sure.

Jim is polishing two guns in the basement. He smiles as I come down the stairs. "How's our heavy sleeper?"

"Sleepy." We both laugh.

"You looked so content when I got up I decided to let you sleep. This farm schedule can easy knock a fellow off a bit."

"Yeah, I guess you're right," I say. But what about my sleepless night? Will Jim understand?

"Want to try your hand at shooting?" he says.

"Sure, why not?" I take the gun and look through the open barrel. "Your mother says you're a pretty good shot."

"Oh, not as good as John was. He hit two birds at a time once."

"No kidding. How'd he do that?"

"These two pheasants went flying out of the cornfield and old John goes up and shoots. One shot and two cockbirds fall to the ground. It was really some story, I'll tell you!" Jim chuckles to himself as he hands me some shells. "Yeah, Two Bird Johnny. That's what they called him at school. But the funny thing was that he didn't get another bird the rest of that season. These guys from school would come here to hunt with us just to see John shoot, and he never got a thing. He took it well, but he finally told them to stop coming."

We join Wilmo at the barn and shoot at the pigeons as they land on the silo. Jim gets at least two but I'm as bad a shot as Wilmo.

As we walk toward the house, I turn to Jim. "I was over at Eli's place last night."

"Yeah, I know," he says. "It sounds like you had a nice time."

"No, Jim, I mean I was over again during the night."

He stops and looks at me. "You were? What for?"

"I had to talk to him, Jim. I can't really explain it. But I guess you could say I'm Christian now. And man, it feels good." I think the smile on my face puzzles him.

"You're putting me on, Eric," he says. "You know, that's really not a very funny joke. Eli's a fine man."

I grab Jim's arm. "I know. That's what I'm saying. He helped me find God. I was over there half the night."

The look on Jim's face is one of surprise and uncertainty. "You're not kidding, are you?" he says.

"No, Jim." I smile. "No, I'm telling you straight. I think I'm a new believer." And even as I say it, I wonder what it means.

6

"You're sure you want to stay here, Eric?"

I nod. "I'll be okay, Jim. Tell Wilson I'm doing my thing here in Pennsylvania if he asks."

"Sure." Jim stands watching the tracks in the cold morning, blowing warm air from his mouth to his nose. He holds the same battered suitcase he brought with him when we came for the funeral.

"You think I'm nuts, don't you?" I ask him. I know he was amazed when I told him yesterday that I wanted to stay on in Pennsylvania, even if he went back to the university.

"No, I don't think you're nuts, Eric. A little crazy maybe, but not nuts," he smiles, blowing on his nose.

"I have to find out for myself, Jim. Something happened to me that night at Eli's place. Something deep in me was touched. Something was healed. I'm not sure it fits the conventional language of your Mennonite community, but I want to try to get it all together before I go back to the city."

"Sure, man. You have my encouragement. It's just that I grew up here and don't find it all that fascinating. And if I don't get back to classes, I'll have to go an extra semester. And I don't want to gamble with that."

He stands looking down the tracks and I watch his face. I can't blame him for wanting to get away from here. His two brothers lie buried high on the hill behind the house they used to make home. Jim is all alone now, and it's beginning to eat at him. His family doesn't understand. They seem to hold him responsible for it all. Somehow Jim should have prevented death from claiming John, their silence seems to say. And Jim says nothing in return. In the week since the funeral he has worked around the farm and tried to help his parents forget the shock of Big John's death. And when their silence accused him of things he would have given his life to prevent, Jim acted as though he didn't hear the silence.

The train whistles in the distance. "To you this is a place of death," I say to Jim, "but for me it's a place of birth."

He nods, his face serious. And as the train comes steaming to a stop, he takes my hand. "You've been a real friend, Eric. I can never thank you as I should."

"You're the one who should be thanked," I say.

He steps aboard. The conductor is shouting up ahead and pulling a lever. The train jerks. Jim turns and looks at me as the train begins to move. "Be careful, Eric," he calls. "Don't expect too much from them. They're just ordinary people."

And then he's gone. The platform is empty and the steam evaporates in the freezing air. Jim is off to the city. And I have stayed behind to learn more about

56

these people. These people and me.

When I get back to the farm, Wilmo is roaring around the barnyard with the tractor, loading manure on the spreader. Mr. Witmer is watching from the barn.

"Train on time?" he asks.

"A little late. But not much." I watch Jim's father as he leans on the bottom half of the door, a piece of hay working back and forth between his teeth. I notice his cheeks are red and clean shaven.

"Wilmer and I were planning to go to the stock-yards this morning, Eric," he says. "Want to go along?"

"Sure, I'd really like that."

"Wilmer's cleaning the barnyard just in case we do buy some steers. I hear the price is pretty good this week," he says, tossing the piece of hay away and turning back into the barn. "We better bed the stables."

I go up the ladder and throw the straw down through the holes into the stables while Jim's father opens the bales and kicks the bedding around the pens as the cattle romp and kick and chew the stuff. I help him with the last few bales. Then we climb out over the bars and he gives me the handful of twine. There's a pipe near the granary where they hang their twine and I take it there, suddenly aware of how much I've learned about the farm in the short time I've been here.

Wilmo is splashing his face at the trough in the entry when I come back. He too has shaven since breakfast. Funny thing how they didn't go along to the station to see Jim off. His mother never even kissed him good-bye. She scolded him the whole meal and when we were getting in the car she called down from the porch and told him to write more often. There was warmth and concern in her tone, but Jim's whole departure was strangely emotionless. Wilmo was still at the table when we left and Jim's father was working at his rolltop desk. Father and son shook hands briefly and that was all. "Must you go back to that sinful place where they killed John?" the old man's eyes seemed to ask. But he said nothing as they shook hands by the desk. He had no words of hope, no words of encouragement and love. And so Jim left this place of death he used to love, alone in his grief. Not bitterly did he leave, like a man vowing to return someday to avenge his brother's blood. For Jim sought not revenge, but peace. Peace and time to heal the wounds.

And now that Jim is gone, I see his parents in a different light. They seek no revenge either. They are confused in the face of death. There are muted questions on their lips. Questions their faith has taught them not to ask. And as the days go by, I see that they do indeed love Jim. And he loves them. In a quiet, long-distance sort of way.

The stockyards stretch for many blocks, pen after pen with endless gates and alleys. Mr. Witmer, in an old plain suit, black hat, and clean boots, goes from pen to pen, conferring now and then with Wilmo, clad in a green work jacket with a big zipper up the front, collar high about the neck, and a cap pulled down over his diminishing crop of hair, proclaiming in big letters the merits of Landis Feeds. They are a timid duo, glancing with big open faces at the other farmers in their stylish hats and coats and whips, trying to smile and managing only a twitch of an eyebrow in a curious sort of self-conscious gesture. Wilmo carries an old cane which he uses to jab the cattle to get them to move about the pen. He talks real loud when no one else is anywhere in sight, as though the cattle don't mind. But when some other men come walking up and ask about the cattle under observation, Wilmo can hardly muster the energy to whisper a reply.

I must confess, of course, that I probably make things worse for them. Most Mennonites and Amish around here, it seems, are used to being considered a little different. They want to be different, in fact. It's all a part of the faith. But I'm different in the wrong way and I get this feeling Wilmo tries to stay up ahead so that people won't think we're together.

We meet a big fellow called Shorty. Mr. Witmer has done business with him before, and he relaxes as Shorty leads us from pen to pen, quoting prices and pointing out the good angles of each offer.

"Now that's what you call a nice bunch of cattle, Menno." He points his cane. "You aren't going to find a better deal than that if you stay here all week."

"How many are there altogether?"

"Seventeen."

Wilmo kicks at the fence with his shoe. "Where are they from?" he asks.

"Virginia."

Menno acts disinterested. "They look too high-priced for me."

"Sure, they look high-priced, Menno. That's the point. That's why they're such a terrific buy. Where else are you going to find another bunch of cattle that looks that fine with a price tag of only thirty-four cents?"

"I can't afford more than twenty-six cents a pound for those there," Menno says, turning away.

"Twenty-six! Be reasonable," Shorty says, walking after him. "How much money do you expect me to lose?"

"Well, Shorty, how about twenty-eight cents? Will you sell for twenty-eight cents?"

Shorty throws up his hands. "I paid more than that for them myself. I won't sell those beauties at a loss. They're too good."

"Well, what else you got?" Menno asks, walking across the alley.

Shorty doesn't give up easily. "Look, Menno, I want to sell you those cattle. I think they're just the ones for you."

"Oh, I have nothing against those cattle," says Menno over his shoulder. "Nothing but the price." His craftiness amazes me.

"Okay. I'll give a little. Thirty-two and a half. But that's the best I can do. How about it?"

Wilmo grunts, walks off with Menno, and leaves Shorty staring at me with pleading eyes. "Honest to God, I paid thirty and a half for those steers," he says.

He shows us several other pens of cattle but farmers Menno and Wilmo exhibit no interest. There are sheep and hogs and calves and cattle of all kind, pen after pen, row after row, just bought and just sold.

But nothing interests these farmers today.

As we are turning to leave, Shorty makes his last offer. "I'll give them to you for thirty-one and a half," he says.

"You mean those seventeen back in that other pen?"

He nods. "Thirty-one and a half."

"I'll tell you what, Shorty," Menno says, stepping up to the stocky cattle dealer and using a confidential tone. "I have a feeling you'll sell for thirty cents. So I'll offer you twenty-eight and a half and we can split the difference."

"Not a chance," Shorty says.

"Well, Wilmer, I guess we better get back to the farm," Menno says. "Maybe some other day, Shorty."

We are almost five pens away when Shorty shouts after us. "Thirty and a half — and that's all."

Menno and Wilmo turn and look back. "I thought we said thirty was the compromise," Jim's father calls. "You always put your price too high, Shorty."

"Okay, take your cattle. I don't want them anyhow."

"Thirty cents?"

"Thirty cents." Shorty waves his agreement halfheartedly.

"It's a pleasure doing business with you, Shorty."

Wilmo laughs as we turn and walk toward the big gate and Mr. Witmer seems pleased with himself. There's a spirit of triumph in their step and they don't twitch at the passing farmers anymore. Shorty said he paid thirty and a half but he sold for thirty. I ask them about it.

61

"They always jack up their price," Menno says. Wilmo agrees. "Yeah, Shorty's a real shyster."

"A what?"

"Shyster. It means a crook or something like that."

We stop at the snack shop near the big gate and buy hot dogs. They eat with big bites in happy celebration of a good morning at the stockyards. Wilmo puts so much catsup on his that it runs out, mixed with the mustard, and drops on the zipper of his new green jacket. He wipes it off with his sleeve.

Menno asks the girl for a glass of water so that he doesn't have to buy a soft drink. She brings a glass for each of us. Wilmo drips some on his zipper, causing a tiny catsup-mustard landslide down his front.

"What would you have done if Shorty wouldn't have accepted your offer?" I ask Mr. Witmer. "Would you have given more money for those cattle?"

"One cent," he smiles, half glowing to himself. "I'd have given him thirty-one cents. They're good cattle, Eric."

We stand in a corner of the smoky joint, sipping our water and listening to the talk of the men. The waitresses are ugly with oily faces and greasy hair just as they are at the truck stops. But the men flirt with them anyhow.

We stop for some groceries on the way home. It seems like a big trip for the farmers, ten miles into town, buying some cattle, eating hot dogs, and stopping at the sprawling supermarket on the way home. It's a small trip, but it reveals so much about Wilmo and the farmer he works for.

We pass through a little town where they've put

up some of their Christmas decorations already. Wilmo laughs in disgust as he points at a dangling star.

"They left them decorations up all summer," he says. "And now they're taking them down to fix them. Probably won't get them back up for Christmas."

A long cattle truck is parked at the barnyard when we get back to the farm. The seventeen are already sniffing their new home. The driver stands on the porch, talking to the farmer's wife. He comes down the steps as we get out of the car.

"I guess that's where you wanted them," he says in a voice much too squeaky for his big body. Wilmo snickers.

Mr. Witmer nods. "My wife took care of you?"

"Sure. They'll mail the bill," says Squeaky.

"Thanks." Jim's father is a smallish man with a smallish voice. He stands with hands in pockets, casually watching the big truck start with a roar and dust its way out the lane, the burly driver squeaking along behind the wheel. "Some rig," he says. Wilmo nods with a shake of the head. Then he spits. "Some driver," he says.

At supper, the farmers tell the farmer's wife all about their big trip to the stockyards. She listens carefully and injects little news bits of her own when she gets a chance. The Zimmerman twins are in the hospital again, Jake and Mary are going to Florida to see their son, and Brother Kauffman from Indiana will be at the Harnishes for supper on Saturday after the harvest service. They hardly notice me. Not that they mean it unkind or anything. We live in different worlds.

The telephone rings as we begin our cherry pie and tapioca. Wilmo answers it.

"Yeah?" he says. He listens for a minute. "Who is this?" He breaks into a smile. "Sure, Eli, I sure will." He comes back to the table, grinning from ear to ear. "It's for you," he says to me.

I leave my pie and take the receiver. "Hello, Eli."

"Hello, Eric. I've been meaning to call you sooner. Will I see you Saturday?"

"Yes, I plan to be there." Eli had asked me to come over to his place Saturday mornings to study the Scriptures.

"Eric, I've been thinking about you a lot this week. And you know, one of the problems with young Christians is that they don't express their faith enough."

"Really?"

"And so I was wondering if you might say a few words at our harvest service Saturday afternoon."

"About what, Eli?"

"About your new walk with God."

I am silent for several long moments. I feel a tremor sweeping through my body and I try to think. What is there to say?

"Well, Eli," I sputter, "how about if we talk it over Saturday morning?"

"Sure, Eric," he says. His voice is kind. "But think it over seriously," he adds. "I believe it'll be good for all of us."

7

Like peasants in a small chapel freshly hewn out of the forest, the worshipers sit in their benches, waiting for the harvest service to begin. The men sit on the left side of the aisle, the women on the right. The church is nearly full.

I sit on a bench near the back, listening to the murmur of the congregation as the clock over the pulpit ticks its hands toward two o'clock. Wilmo told me on Sunday that the clock used to be on the side wall in the old church, and he liked it better that way. Not so noticeable, he said. And it's true, the clock isn't exactly hard to see, hanging there above the simple desk.

The day is perfect for thanksgiving. The bright sun slants through the clear windows, warming the walls and touching the farmers and their wives and children as they sing out their praise in lusty, unaccompanied hymnody. The stark simplicity of these people and their chapel is not so stark and not so easily understood when their singing fills their humble meetinghouse. There's something holy and something mystic about it all. The harvest may not have been as good as other years, but there's enough for all. And so they sing their praise. And something in their tone convinces me that they would sing if there had been no crops to gather in at all. It's the way of the faith.

As I listen to them sing, I feel in a small way, for the first time since I left the city, that maybe I belong. Not in a big way, of course, but in a warm way. Maybe it's because I finally cut my hair and people don't stare at me so much anymore. But I think it's more. Something in me that needed healing was touched, and I'm not sure of all the words and everything, but something in their singing makes me believe that these people, too, have been touched. At least some.

Eli is standing in the pulpit now, his smile spreading among his sheep. He is telling them that I have recently found a new birth of faith. "I'm overjoyed about Eric's new discovery," he says. "What better way is there to give thanks than to hear the testimony of a new believer? And so I've asked him if he'd read the Scripture for us and give us a few words of his own."

When he first asked me over the phone, it scared me a lot. But as the time came nearer, I really thought it wouldn't be too bad. Eli and I talked about it this morning and he helped me choose some Scripture.

But now as I stand up and walk toward the front, my throat goes dry, my palms begin to sweat, and my feet on the hard wood of the new floor create a thunder in the little church. Step after step, eyes turning toward me in serious, curious stares. Men and women both. Children too.

I can't believe I'm so nervous. Man, I've appeared on stage in front of audiences ten times the size of this small congregation. So why the butterflies? Why the fear?

I stand before them, speechless and tense, the Bible open in my hands to the chosen passage. And then I begin to understand my fear.

"There was darkness and now there is light," I say at last. And I'm amazed how calm it sounds. "There was despair and now there is hope. There was hatred and now there is love."

And then my mind goes blank. I can't remember the words. For a moment I want to rush from this plain sanctuary, away from the gaze of these plain people and their simple lives. For that's the fear that stops my tongue. Not fear of speaking, not fear of being watched. Nor is it fear of confessing faith in a miracle I can't explain or understand.

The fear that dries my mouth as I stand before these Mennonites is more complex than that. And far beyond my reach. It strikes deep at my very center and chills my heart.

My fear is that these people won't accept me. Sooner or later we all face that fear, I guess. But it's never so humiliating and disarming as when the ones who do the rejecting are simple farmers who know almost nothing about anything. Or so it seems.

How long I stand there mute with fear I'm not quite sure. Then all of a sudden I'm reading the Scripture and I'm just as cool as can be. I even smile between verses. The fear is gone. At least for the moment.

We kneel for silent prayer. And in the hush, I pray the impossible. "O God," I breathe, "take the fear away." And after meditating for a moment, I add, "If they do reject me, show me the way of love."

When I get back to my bench, I slump down a bit, self-conscious of my awkward performance. But no one seems to notice. They're singing another rousing hymn and I sing along. Maybe it's all in my head.

Across the aisle, two benches front, I see Hazel glance my way as the hymn concludes. She smiles, and her eyes seem to be telling me something.

Brother Kauffman, it turns out, is a disappointment. His sermon is filled with truisms and disconnected phrases. But the people don't appear to mind much. The men in front of me take turns napping.

It's hard to explain how I feel as the service comes to a close. There's something in the faith and way of life of these people that struck me the moment I arrived as being pure and true and godly. But I keep realizing how inconsistent and provincial these same people really are. Do they seem honest and good because they live in the seventeenth century? Or is there something really special about them?

It all sounds silly, I guess. But it's real, too. And there's no one here with whom I can discuss these questions that surge back and forth in my veins. No one understands.

The social part of the service begins as soon as the benediction is pronounced. The men in front of me turn around in their bench and shake hands with each other, exchanging greetings and bits of friendly gossip almost as though I'm not there.

"Afternoon, Noah," the skinny one says, shaking hands with the fat-cheeked farmer in the brown suit. His blond hair is cut so close it's hard to tell which is hair and which is head.

"Leonard," nods short-haired Noah. Leonard turns to the man with the glasses.

"How are you, Mel?"

"Oh, just okay, I guess. How's Leonard?"

They shake. "Fine. Say, Mel, I hear your milkman had a little trouble with your fence the other day."

"Yeah, the dumb guy," grins the glasses. "He said his brakes weren't so hot."

Noah is the only one who notices me. Twice he glances at me timidly from under his close-cut stubble. Finally he ventures his hand. "Hi," he says, "my name is Noah Dombach."

I smile. "I'm Eric."

"Yeah, I know," he says, spreading his fat cheeks into a smile. "I saw you here Sunday, only you looked a little different then. Wasn't that you?"

"I was with Jim Witmer."

"Yeah, I thought so," he says, eyes earnest. "He went back to college, now didn't he?"

I nod. "Yes, he did." It seems as though Noah has me figured out.

"You're the one who used to be a hippie, right?" he says, casually slipping his hands into his big brown pockets. But he doesn't wait for an answer. "I guess that's an awful life, isn't it?"

I look at him for a moment without answering, trying to understand what he's getting at. "I wasn't exactly what you'd call a hippie."

"Oh, you weren't," he says, disappointment heavy in his voice. "They said you were." He stares at me awkwardly for a bit, then turns and follows the others out of the church. "See you around," he says.

"Sure, Noah." I turn to go. Several of the older men shake my hand and tell me they're glad I could come. And one of the women comes across the aisle as I'm about to go out the back door.

"I'm Mrs. William Sauder," she says, "and I just wanted you to know how pleased we are that you found the Lord. If you just trust in Him, everything will work out for good." She holds a crying child in her arms as she goes on, her eyes moving as fast as her tongue. "Why, I was just saying to William last night that we don't depend on the Lord enough. And a person like you, from your background, especially needs to stay close to the Lord," she goes on, "or the evil one will snatch you away. I told William I really pity people like you." She stops abruptly. "Eli's a wonderful man, isn't he?" She beams, her child screaming louder than ever.

"Yes," I say in a quiet voice, hoping the baby will settle down. "Yes, Eli's a fine man."

"See you some more," she says, turning and walking down the stairs with her unhappy child. Several women stand near the door, watching. "Susie never trains her children," the short one complains. The others nod their agreement. But Susie doesn't hear. She's already begun her tongue assault on the old man with the hearing aid at the foot of the stairs.

I'm almost at the car when Hazel comes walking up. I haven't talked to her since that night in her

70

bedroom. She wears a new coat and a happy face.

"Hello, Hazel," I say, a bit self-consciously.

"Hello, Eric." Her voice has a light, bursting quality about it.

"You're looking lively today," I tell her.

"I feel lively," she smiles. Her manner has an unusual touch of secrecy and intrigue.

"What's new?" I ask as nonchalantly as possible.

"Everything," she answers and her tone has that ripple in it again. "We're having a hayride tonight, and I thought you might enjoy going along."

"Who's we?"

"The young people from the church. We invited some other youth groups."

"What time?"

"Eight o'clock at Roger Martin's place."

I watch her closely as she speaks, trying to weigh the invitation, wondering if she really wants me to come. But if she's keeping secrets, her attractive face doesn't show a trace of it. Perhaps I'm crediting her with more perception than she really has.

"Thanks for the invitation," I say, trying to sound congenial and tentative at the same time. "I might be there."

"I'll be looking for you," she says. "I like hayrides." She teases her lips into a gentle smile. It's there and then it's not. And then she turns and walks away.

I'm sure all Mennonites are not as simple as Noah Dombach and some of the others here at the harvest service. Eli certainly is not. Nor are Jim's folks. But Hazel seems such a contrast to the other young people. She keeps amazing me with the diversity of her personality. And I find her just as intriguing and unpredictable as many of the girls I knew in the city.

Roger Martin's place is hidden away among the hills, and the narrow winding country roads somehow don't want to lead me there. When I finally find the mailbox and follow the long bumpy lane to the farm buildings down beside the pond, the wagons are loaded and the tractors are ready, lights blazing and engines roaring. The riders send up a shout as the caravan begins to move. I park on the upper bank and jump out quickly. I run toward the moving lights, wondering which wagon to choose. And then I hear her voice calling me, with that same bright cheery playfulness. I turn and run toward her as she calls, my eyes blinded by the headlights.

"Over here, Eric!"

I shield my eyes and look across the wagon, full of people in bright blankets, sitting in the piles of hay. Near the back, on the other side of the moving float of people, Hazel is waving at me. I dart across, between the wagon and the next tractor. She takes my hand as I struggle to climb aboard, careful of the wheel at my feet. For a minute I'm scared I won't make it. But my foot gets a grip on the ledge of the sideboard and I tumble on board, headfirst.

The wagon is crowded and it takes me a while to get myself right side up. I never have been athletic, especially not with my head all tangled up in loose piles of hay. Hazel laughs at me as I crawl out from the feet and blankets, shaking the hay from my head.

She pulls me to her side, brushing the hay from my collar and tucking her blanket around my legs. "You almost missed the train," she says.

"I'm never taking directions from Wilmo again," I grumble, still working myself into the hay. The couple beside me seem to be snuggled together about as closely as possible; so I settle for the little space in the corner beside Hazel.

"Did you get lost?" she asks, her musical voice close to my ear as I push the hay into the corner.

"Do I seem lost?" I ask as I settle back beside her, the blanket tight around our legs. She slips her hand in mine.

"No, you don't seem lost," she murmurs, "but you do act a little scared."

"Scared!" I squeeze her hand and laugh. Sure, Hazel is a lovely lady. And she is disarmingly direct and witty. But I've met her kind many times before — and we weren't just holding hands either. Wow! Who does this sheltered virgin think she is, anyhow? Maybe she can hypnotize little country boys, but she'd better think twice before she assumes she's got me in the palm of her hand. Figuratively speaking, that is.

"Oh, I know you're not scared of me," she says teasingly as we roar along the narrow country road. "You're scared of them."

"And who's them?"

Her eyes pass from couple to couple, snuggled together under their blankets, singing, laughing, shouting, and making love. "Them," she says, her face serious and her voice almost sad. "Most people think

73

we're just a bunch of dumb, retarded hicks. Tourists treat us that way. Thank God we don't have many of them in these parts. They stick to the main roads and the densely settled Amish areas. My Uncle Joe says they trample all over his farm." She pulls her hand away from mine, her eyes full of anger. "But tourists aren't the worst. It's the Mennonites who think they're really modern and liberal who really make me mad. They walk around with their heads in the clouds, trying to act like the world and looking down on us as though we're some kind of weird prehistoric creatures."

Hazel falls silent, and for a long moment we listen to the singing and the laughter and watch the moonlight in the stream along the road zigzag among the trees. Our blanket is warm and I can feel her shoulder rise and fall with her breathing as she stares out across the night.

"Most of us are farmers," she says, her voice mellow with confession, "but farmers are people, too. And people are people the world around. That's what outsiders don't understand." She smiles to herself. "It's when they try to join us that they have to face the truth," she says.

The caravan of tractors and wagons has reached the top of the hill, and as we go roaring down the other side, the riders send up another cheer. Hazel joins in the excitement, screaming with the others as we rush toward the crest of the hill and the corner at the bottom. She grabs my hand as the cold wind chills us and I slip my arm around her, pulling her warm soft body close to mine. The corner is a sharp one, and as we speed around it, roaring like a bunch of kids on a roller coaster, Hazel comes spilling into my lap. It's my turn to laugh as I hold her there for a moment, struggling in my arms, embarrassed and indignant. "I think I like hayrides, too," I chuckle in her ear.

"Let me go," she demands, digging her fingers into my legs.

"Say please."

She struggles for a while, trying to untangle her skirts. But I hold her tight. Finally she relaxes, leaning against me, and whispers in my ear. "I didn't make you say please," she says, her voice teasing and warm.

She rests in my arms for a long moment, our bodies entangled under the blanket in a momentary caress. "You don't need to be scared of us, Eric," she says. "We might even learn to like you, if you don't try to analyze us all the time."

She pulls herself gently away, brushing my cheek with her lips as she settles back beside me. And I just sit there, trying to understand what she means by it all.

75

8

Rufus is a different kind of Mennonite. He's always in a rush, talking, planning, and making deals, speeding away in his Continental to some big board meeting or important convention. He wears the latest in clothes, half a season behind New York's latest, but sensationally "in" around here. Rufus owns a chocolate factory, a series of filling stations, an egg processing plant, and a dozen farms which produce the lush, fresh vegetables he sells here at Green Thumb Market. And as if that doesn't make him tycoon enough, he also sits on several Mennonite church boards and mission agencies.

Rufus has a big interest in saving souls. It doesn't take long to find that out. Only it strikes me sort of funny the way he talks about it. He's totally different from Eli. Somehow there's something superficial about his enthusiasm. Or maybe I get him all wrong. First impressions often are that way.

I sit in his office, plush with thick carpet and expensive paneling. I listen as he tells me how happy he is that I have come to the Lord. I wonder what he means. But I have no chance to speak. Between explaining how glad he is to be able to offer me a job here at Green Thumb and telling me how busy his schedule has been these past days, what with that Puerto Rican giving him a little trouble and all, I never really do find out the conditions of my employment. How much do I get paid, what are the exact hours, how much insurance coverage comes with the job, and how many vacation days per month can I expect? Nothing. He says nothing about any of these things. Somehow they don't quite matter.

Jim's mother was the one who suggested her brother might be able to get me a job. It wasn't hard to see that she and he live in different worlds, even though Green Thumb is only five miles from the Witmer farm. Rufus was worldly, she seemed to be saying, but he may have some work for me. The farm work was slackening up with the coming of November.

Rufus summons Stanley the foreman into the office. Stanley has the ears of a small elephant and the face of a raccoon.

"I got a new man for you," Rufus says.

"That's good," Stanley enthuses with a coony smile. "We're really going to be short of help from here to Christmas. The Thanksgiving rush has already begun."

Rufus seems pleased. "We always like to hear that they're buying the stuff faster than we can put it on the shelves." He looks at me. "This is Eric, Stanley. He used to be a hippie but Eli helped him find the Lord and he's in the church now. So we're glad to have him."

"I should say we are," Stanley agrees, his big eyes looking me over, ears pointed and alert. "You come with me, Eric."

I start toward the door, amazed how being a hippie can sound so undesirable. Almost as queer as being a Mennonite or Amish. I never thought of it that way before. Hazel and I may have more in common than we think!

"Oh, Eric," Rufus calls after me, "we'd like to have you out to our church one of these Sundays and hear all about your conversion." He is already dialing on the phone. "Our church is a little more modern than Eli's." There's a tone of smug condescension in his observation.

Stanley talks a lot. "So you used to be a flower child?" he asks in his loud baritone as we go down the steps.

"Maybe I still am," I say.

He stops in mid-step, as though he's got some air brakes hidden away in his legs someplace, and thrusts his raccoon features into my face. "What?" he says, disbelief in his pale brown eyes, "are you a Christian hippie?"

I smile at him. "What's so strange about that?"

He ponders. "I've heard a lot about these long-haired hippies who burn banks and blow up buildings," he says. "Christians don't do that. People must be possessed to do such things."

He shows me the time clock in the back room and tells me all about the aprons and caps employees have to wear. He gives me an application and tells me the procedures for completing the necessary forms. "Rufus is pretty tough about this stuff," he says.

He tells me to help the cashiers pack the purchases the rest of the day since there's a lot of business.

78

"Drop the forms through the slot in my office when you're finished," he says.

He stops by the door. "I'm not a Mennonite," he says. "But Rufus and I get along real well just the same. I'm Assemblies of God myself." He looks at me. "Incidentally, you were kidding about being a Christian hippie, weren't you?"

"There's a lot of people appreciate nature, you know," I say.

"Nature? Oh, sure. Why, I like to go hunting myself." He chuckles from earlobe to earlobe and I can see he's relieved. Somehow it's all very ridiculous. I've never considered myself a hippie in the first place. And furthermore, I'm not sure I even know any hippies. It's such an overused term that it has no meaning anymore. Most people seem to use it for persons they dislike, especially if they're free and young.

I chuckle along with Stanley. "Hunting nature can be a lot of fun," I say.

It doesn't take me long to decide that packing bags while people wait impatiently is not a lot of fun. The produce is beautiful, though. And the prices are really reasonable.

The lunch Jim's mother packed me takes a lot of chewing, like any packed lunch, but the chewing's good. Bologna, the Dutch kind. And homemade cupcakes.

I eat with the others in the lunchroom in the basement. A number of the clerks are Mennonite girls in long dresses with white coverings on their heads. The rest are a bunch of farmerish-looking young men with lunch buckets, probably Mennonites too. Except for the two "suave" cats talking to the girl in the mini-skirt by the water cooler.

"You mean you're really going skiing in Vermont with Rufus?" the pale boy in the purple shirt and tie combination is asking the girl.

"That's what he said," she gushes, her eyebrows arched with an air of superiority.

The boys in the cool threads move in closer, their eyes roving her body as she crosses her legs and sips on her coffee. They try to whisper so that the others won't hear. "And his wife isn't going along?" they ask, mouths open as if to suck in the news.

"Why don't you nosy little boys get back to your bookkeeping?" The girl smiles, her homeliness undisguised by her short skirt and the abundance of cosmetics. But the suave boys think she's cute. They stand leaning over her, waiting and looking like over-size schoolboys hungry for a lollipop.

"Look, Carolyn, we tell you everything," the purple shirt insists.

"Of course you do," Carolyn scoffs. "All day long I've got to listen to your mouth. But what you got to tell ain't worth a nickel." She stands up and gives them a meaningful look. "Maybe that's why you don't get invited to Vermont by the boss. And maybe that's why you don't learn all the details about the people who do get invited." She turns abruptly and struts from the room like an ugly duckling showing off new tail feathers. Only her pantyhose is sagging at the knees a little more with every jaunty step. The bookkeepers watch her every move.

80

"Boy, she gets in on everything," admires the one with the wrinkled pocket handkerchief. The purple shirt nods vigorously, his face blushing in the afterglow of their encounter. They giggle momentarily, lost in the excitement of their own little mystery story. Then they hurry from the room, doubtless in pursuit of the mini-skirt and the cosmetics and the secrets that make their boring job so worthwhile.

The Mennonite girls ignored the whole episode. But the boys sat in their corner, eating and talking and watching Carolyn out of the corner of their eyes.

"The silly thing," grunts the red-haired guy with the suspenders after the trio is gone. "She is really a big mouth if I ever saw one."

"You said it, Mark," one of the older men agrees.

"You think Rufus will take her along without his wife?" asks Tim, the guy who works at the meat counter.

"It's a bunch of hot air," Mark answers. "Rufus ain't that dumb. That girl just thinks she's hot stuff since Rufus made her his secretary. But she's nothing but a big bunch of bologna."

"You keep her out of my department," Tim says. "She's worse than bologna." They laugh, and we all go back to work.

When I get home to Witmers, I give Hazel a call. "Mind if I run over for a while this evening?" I ask her.

"Hey, that's a good idea," she says. "I have some work to do, though. Papa has to study for his sermons this weekend in Ohio."

"Well, maybe I better not come — "

"Eric, I'd like you to come," she says. "Maybe I'll put you to work, but you're not scared of that, are you?" She laughs.

"I'm not Mennonite enough to keep up with you, Hazel. But if you let me work at my own pace, maybe — "

"Oh, shut up," she retorts, her voice full of teasing. "You're just plain lazy."

"Sure. Next thing you'll call me a hippie, just like the others."

"Oh, stop feeling sorry for yourself, Eric. Working at Green Thumb can't be that bad."

"I'll be there at seven, Hazel."

"Good. I'll make a list of work," she says, laughing. And the conversation has turned a boring day of packing bags for grumpy customers into the promise of a relaxing November evening with the nicest girl in Pennsylvania.

Mrs. Witmer wants to know about Green Thumb. "Rufus treat you okay?" she asks as she works by the sink.

"Yeah, I even saw his office," I tell her. "He's a pretty important man the way it sounds."

"That's what they say." The lines in her face relax and she smiles, revealing a faint sort of pride in her brother. "He never did very well in school, you know. But he was always full of curiosity about things. I guess that's why he does so well in business."

"Yeah, I guess he's pretty rich."

"Oh, I don't know," she says. But I can see that she does know. She puts some pies into the oven.

"Rufus doesn't quite seem like a lot of the Mennonites around here," I say, half to myself and half to her. I see the smile go out of her eyes. For a long moment she just looks at me, trying to decide what to say. Then she sits at the table, and for the first time I hear from the real Anna Witmer.

"Rufus never learned to be obedient," she says, and there is a sadness in her almost angry tone. "He was the youngest in our family and he was forever giving Father a heartache. He got mixed up with the wrong crowd, I guess. He never came to church anymore and he was always rude at home. He was just a selfish boy, that's all I can figure."

She sighs. "Rufus even went to dances and movies. Mother thought it couldn't be. But then one day he straightened up. He went to some meetings up at Shepherd Hill and I guess he was changed. They're the real liberal Mennonites, you know," she says, "and it's a sin some of the things they do at that church — the way they dress and stuff. But I've got to admit, they helped Rufus."

She checks the oven and starts washing dishes. "Father was glad he was changed, but he was upset that Rufus kept going up there to Shepherd Hill. And when Rufus married Louise, my parents wouldn't hear of it. But Rufus got married just the same. Two of my brothers went to the wedding, that was all." She washes in silence for a moment. "I often wonder if I should have gone," she says, and she looks at me, her eyes troubled and sad.

"Of course, we get along pretty well now," she adds. I watch her gaze out through the window above the sink, far off to the little graveyard on the hill, half hidden in the early November dusk. And for a moment I see a wish in her face — a wish that her sons would come home. A wish in the face of a mother. Answered by silence and night as the darkness envelops the hill. But Anna keeps all these things in her heart. "It's getting dark," she says, and the yearning is gone from her voice.

Wilmo is very talkative at supper, asking all about Green Thumb and the people who work there. Jim's father listens, eating the mush and milk in his usual silence. And Mrs. Witmer keeps him company.

Hazel is wiping her hands on her apron as she opens the door and invites me in. Several children sit around the table with schoolbooks in front of them. And Eli is by the desk, talking on the telephone. She takes my coat and guides me to the sink. "Did you ever clean carrots?" she asks, handing me a paring knife with a mischievous grin.

"I happen to like carrots," I grin back at her, "but I can't work without an apron!"

We work at carrots for nearly an hour. Thirteen people take a lot of food. I cut my finger and get a little red in the orange.

Eli drops by the sink to chat a bit. He tells me he's going back to his home community in Ohio for some weekend meetings. "I promised them almost two years ago," he says, "and I'm really anxious to go. But it is a long trip."

"Yeah, I hitchhiked the whole way from Chicago to Philadelphia one time. It's a long way."

Eli lays a gentle hand on my shoulder. "I was

thinking, Eric, that maybe I could persuade you to go with me."

"Me?" I turn and look at him, and see that the lines in his face are serious. "You mean it, don't you?"

He nods. I turn to Hazel. "Are you going?"

"I'm playing mother this weekend," she smiles. "Next weekend is my turn."

"Okay, it's a deal," I say, wiping my hands on my bloody apron and glancing at Hazel. "I'll go to Ohio this weekend, and maybe next weekend — "

"That's pretty far away," Hazel interrupts with a twinkle in her eye. "I seldom plan that far ahead."

9

Weeks pass. Thanksgiving comes and goes. Carolyn goes skiing in Vermont with Rufus and Louise and some of the other swinging Mennonites, causing a murmur among the clerks at Green Thumb, part curiosity and part disapproval. I never went skiing myself; so I don't really care that much.

The "spirit" of Christmas begins where the turkeys and pumpkins leave off. And the shoppers are more impatient than ever. I still pack bags a lot. Sometimes I get to help Tim with the meats. My English major doesn't seem to help me very much. I end up with mainly uneventful manual chores. And the pay's really not that hot.

Hazel makes it worth the effort. We spend more and more time together. Mostly good. Every so often she gets a dose of independence, especially when I want her most. She can be a stubborn lady. But when I'm not expecting it, she's as darling as can be. Sometimes she's like a child, happy, uninhibited, and charmingly full of adventure.

One warmish Sunday afternoon we ride horseback for miles, gathering old leaves with their rained-off colors and crispy variations. Another time we go singing for old people with some of her friends from church, and I watch the way she touches them, lighting little fires in the vacant eyes of those old, withered faces, hollow and colorless in the loneliness of death. She touches them like a child comforting an old man, lost in a gathering fog, and brings them in from the cold. And when the others turn to go, she lingers by the door of the dreary old building, her eyes passing from bed to bed. "They call it a rest home," she says. "It's a terrible shame the way the children of these people send them here to die." And then I see the woman in the child. The tears in her eyes belong to the child, but the anger belongs to the woman. Hazel growing up.

And then there's Eli. I see him several times a week. Often we study the Scriptures together, reading, talking, and sharing our lives. I read the Bible more and more as time goes on. It's so beautiful, full of poetry and mystery and life. And Eli lives and walks with God. So our times together are precious.

The weekend in Ohio sort of broke the ice, I guess. Eli arranged for me to speak to some of the youth, and we had a good time together. They were quite different from the kids back at Eli's church, but they had a provincial innocence that was much the same. They asked a lot of questions and I think that was when I realized for the first time how easy it would be to shock them by telling them the vivid details of my life. The temptation was great.

And as the weekend passed, I sensed a sort of hero worship from the kids. They hung on every word I said, as though I were some sort of space traveler come home to tell my tales. Only the things they asked about were not my faith or the healing of spirit which I told them God had given. It was the stories from New York they wanted to hear. Just how sinful had the world become, their questions seemed to ask. Tell us every detail of the terrible wicked city. Obviously that was more exciting to them than the story of my faith. But I played it down, telling them I enjoyed the city and wanted to go back someday.

"You probably know all about dope, don't you?" a little blond asked me, her lovely eyes big with the thought of it all.

"I'm not an expert on drugs," I told her casually. Somehow the whole thing sounded absurd. These white sheltered Mennonite kids wanted to know where it's at! But how could they begin to understand unless they'd lived through the whole bag of modern man? And they couldn't learn that in a day, either.

Wow. That was exactly what Hazel had told me about the Mennonites. "Some people think they can crash right in on us, take a few pictures, ask some dumb questions, and then act like experts on the whole subject of Mennonite faith and culture!" I remember having laughed at her because she didn't often use such big phrases. But she wasn't in the laughing mood. "They can't learn it in a day," she had said. "It takes years, and then they're lucky if they understand."

That weekend in Ohio Eli preached some of the best sermons I've ever heard. He told about the shepherd and his sheep. And it was as vivid as could be. And the people responded. Sort of like sheep.

As the weeks pass, I am invited to other churches on Sunday morning, Sunday evening, and even during the week to "give my testimony." I make a lot of friends. Mennonites have their differences, just like any other ethnic group. And as I travel around, I become aware of more and more of the peculiarities. One congregation is having trouble finding a new pastor. Another is breaking apart over an unheard-of divorce by one of its prominent members. Others I find unique for their emphasis on singing, prayer groups, or missionary work. Each locality seems to have its own family names and traditions. But friendly hands reach out to welcome me in every congregation I visit.

Hazel is not impressed with my popularity. She doesn't object, but there's something protective in her that reaches out and tries to keep me from her people. I can't explain it, but it's there. She goes along with me to some of the churches, but often she stays home. Her family needs her, of course, but it's more than that. It's as though she's scared I'll stumble or embarrass her people somehow. But we never talk about it.

We have some good times with the youth group. "Harold and Elsie Garman are planning to move to an old house near the church," Hazel tells me on the phone one evening early in December. "Harold has trouble with his heart and the youth group wants to help them get their new home ready so the moving won't be such a strain. Lonnie Groff says several of the rooms should be painted and the kitchen and basement need some cleaning."

So we come with buckets, mops, paintbrushes, and old clothes, with the joyful noise of corporate goodwill. Lonnie asks me to help paint the living room with four other guys. There's a lot of cleaning to be done before we can paint. So we call in some of the girls and tell them to get to work. Or rather, I should say a short guy with four big dimples calls in the girls and tells them what to do. They call him Dimp.

"Come on, Becky, let's see you scrub that wall," he says.

"Yes, Dimp," she laughs, making a face at him. "What are you going to do?"

"Me? I'm giving orders." There's a firmness that underlies his comic manner, and the girls giggle as they go about their work.

"Hey, Sam, bring a broom in here," shouts a loud-mouthed, big-boned girl wearing a big patched apron.

"Get your own broom, Sara," Sam shouts back.

Sara stamps her foot in melodramatic protest. She glances around, trying to get the attention of the other boys. But they avoid her eyes, talking real loud about how Mel Martin's milkman backed his truck into the barnyard fence again.

"He is really the dumbest driver I ever saw," Mel's son is saying. "Last time he said it was his brakes. This time he said his tire must have slipped on the manure." He laughs. "Pop said he was probably a little drunk."

Sara rushes over and sticks her patched apron into the middle of the conversation. "Was he really drunk?" she asks, eyes darting from face to face.

Mel, Jr., acts as though it's nothing. "Probably," he

says. Clearly this is something for the men to talk over. The women can listen if they don't ask questions.

"So he was drunk! I've often thought he might be one of those," Sara confides in her loud, flush-it-all-out manner. "He's our milkman too, you know. I remember one time about a year ago I looked in his truck while he was loading the milk in the back. And I saw a bottle on the front seat. I'm sure of it."

Dimp comes walking up. "Sara, how about having a look at that wall? We'd like to finish painting before the milkman comes tomorrow morning." Everyone laughs and a frustrated blush climbs into the big girl's cheeks.

"All I asked for was a broom," she says, her voice suddenly full of pain and pouting. The laughter freezes in the air and she walks back to her bucket. There's a tension in the room as she stands there, confused and hurt. She looks at me.

"Will you get me a broom, mister?" she asks quietly.

"I'll get it," Dimp says, starting toward the door.

"No, Dimple-face. You stay here and play comedian." She points toward me. "This man is the only one who didn't laugh at me," she says. "I want him to get my broom."

Dimp looks at me and I look at Sara. "I'll be glad to," I tell her. She smiles.

Hazel walks in the kitchen door as I come searching for the broom. She's carrying a bag of food.

"Straight from Green Thumb, I'll bet," I say, sniffing.

"No," she grins, "not this time. Hoovers in town are having a special, and it's cheaper."

"Hoovers!" I exclaim. "Of course their stuff is cheaper. It's half rotten."

"No food for you," she warns me.

"You look nice in boots," I tell her. And she does.

"You do too," she says, laughing at my feet.

"Wilmo told me everyone around here wears these. Only I haven't seen another pair like them since I got here," I complain.

"Papa has some just like them," she says, "only they're worse."

I tell her about Sara. "Yeah, she's like that," Hazel says. "Don't let it bother you. But be nice to her. I'll tell you about it sometime."

"About what?"

She takes me aside. "Sara's father took his life last winter. And she's never been the same since then. The youth group isn't as considerate as they should be sometimes."

"You mean her father committed suicide?"

She nods, and I sense her projecting that protectiveness again.

"In other words, they're not Mennonites?"

There's a pain in Hazel's eyes, but she doesn't look away. "No," she says in a level tone, "they belong to our church. Sara and I were pretty good friends, in fact. They live only about two miles from our place."

"But what happened?"

Her eyes narrow. "What are you, some kind of investigator?" she snaps. "I told you to be kind to her.

And asking questions and being kind don't go together."

"I get your point, Hazel." It almost makes me angry. Who does she think she is, protecting everybody?

She brings me a broom. "I'm sorry," I tell her. "I didn't mean to be vicious."

"None of us do," she says, squeezing my hand.

I hurry across the hall and look for Sara in the living room which is crowded fuller than ever.

"Over here, mister," she calls. She's standing part way up a ladder, brushing a crevice. "What takes you so long?"

"I'm sorry, Sara," I say, handing her the broom.

She's startled. "How'd you know my name?"

"I don't know — others used it, I guess."

She smiles. "You're Eric, aren't you?"

I nod and brace myself for the whole hippie line of questioning.

"I like you," she says. "You don't laugh at people." She looks down at me uncertainly for a moment, studying my face. "Let's work together," she says. I remember Hazel's admonition. "Sounds exciting," I say.

Sara and I work together most of the evening, holding the ladder for each other, mopping, sweeping, and washing. About nine o'clock Lonnie announces food for all, upstairs in the empty bedrooms. We sit around the bare walls in our boots and old clothes, talking and laughing at Dimp. Sara doesn't say much. She watches me a lot, in a relaxed sort of happy way. It makes me feel good.

Two of the older youths bring in their guitars and play for us. Mostly gospel songs. The kids begin to tap their feet and sing along in their strong, nasal voices. It really gets pretty loud in the little empty rooms.

I see Hazel watching me to see if I'm singing. I grin at her. She probably thinks I don't know what's happening, but that's where she's wrong. I had a black roommate my first year in college who just about lost his mind listening to Mahalia Jackson and other gospel stars. He liked soul music, too. But every so often it was gospel from morning till morning. And you can't help learning the stuff in that kind of atmosphere.

About the time they begin asking for requests, I get this real strong urge to play. They've done a few folk numbers and all of a sudden I wish I had brought my guitar along. But they probably wouldn't know any of the music I play, anyhow.

"I bet you play the guitar," Sara shouts over the music, leaning toward me with her big earnest face.

"What makes you say that?" I yell above the din.

"I was watching your fingers," she calls back. Smart girl. I guess I was strumming unconsciously.

When they bring the popcorn around the second time, Sara motions to Lonnie. "Did you know Eric plays the guitar?" she asks the youth leader. He looks at me. "No, I didn't," he says, "but I think he should play a number or two before we have our business meeting. How about it, Eric?"

The guitar isn't the best I've ever seen but that doesn't matter. They sit around in their long dresses and boots and listen as I play a little Simon and Garfunkel. I try not to come on too strong. I see Hazel smiling, half surprised and half pleased. And to my amazement, most of the kids begin to hum along. Simon and Garfunkel have even made it with the Mennonites!

I sing another and another. It's the first I've played since Jim and I buried Big John that rainy day on the hill. And the strumming feels good. It soothes and warms me as I look from youth to youth, and it makes me feel at home. It's one of the best experiences I've had among these people, and I'm glad.

Lonnie runs the business meeting. They discuss plans for finishing the painting for Harold and Elsie. Dimp invites the group to his place for a skating party, "as soon as the pond freezes good." Then they talk about their Christmas program.

"I want us to really put on a good program for the whole church this year," Lonnie says.

"Sure," one of the younger girls says, "but it gets so boring. I wish we could do something really new for a change."

"Like what, Esther?"

"I don't know. But all we always seem to do is sing a bunch of carols and stuff, and then read the Scripture about Christmas. There has to be something more meaningful. I really don't have anything in mind, but I wish it would be more exciting."

"Amen," chimes Mel, Jr.

"Anybody got any ideas?" Lonnie asks.

They come up with about ten suggestions, but they're basically the same type of thing. "I wish we could put a new spirit into Christmas," Sara says.

Then it strikes me. I weigh it back and forth in my mind for a moment, trying to anticipate their reaction. But I have no idea how it will strike them. So I just blurt it out.

"How about doing a little play?" I ask.

"A play? About what?"

"About the spirit and meaning of Christmas," I say.

There's silence. Then one by one they begin to shake their heads. "That's a great idea," Esther enthuses.

Hazel doesn't participate in the discussion and I can't tell what she's thinking. She just listens in silence.

"Could you help us get something together?" Lonnie asks me after the majority have voiced their support.

"I'd be glad to."

Esther turns to Hazel. "What about the ministers and trustees? Will they care?"

Hazel measures her words. "We've never done anything like this before, Esther. It could be a great experience. But I'm sure we should ask the ministers for their approval before we go ahead."

"But will we get their approval, Hazel?" Sara asks.

"I have no idea. But I think it's worth a try." The prophet's daughter smiles.

It's going toward eleven o'clock and as the meeting breaks up and they all gather their buckets, brushes, and mops, Sara takes my arm. "I think God sent you," she says.

Wow. That's the first time anyone said that to me.

10

It's a beautiful morning. The snow stopped falling
sometime during the night and the temperature is
dropping by the minute. Dimp calls before I leave for
work and tells me the ice skating party at his place is
on for tonight.

Anna's even happy this morning. She sings softly
to herself by the stove as I talk to Dimp, and she's
rather talkative when the men come in for breakfast.

"I want to go and help Mother put in a quilt this
afternoon," she tells her husband as he rubs his
hands by the stove.

"Is Mother Metzler doing quilts already?" he asks.

"This will be her third one, Menno."

Wilmo is having trouble with a running nose. "Boy,
she makes some of the neatest quilts I've ever seen,"
he says between handkerchiefs. "You ought to see
them, Eric."

"I would love to see how you make them sometime," I say. Jim's mother smiles, a relaxed happiness
I don't often see on her serious face.

"Maybe we can work that out," she says.

The car starts at the first turn of the key. It's
Jim's ancient 1959 model that he said I could use

while he's gone. He calls it "the old flipper."

As I park the old flipper in the back corner of the Green Thumb lot, Stanley comes out the rear door of the store and waves at me. I turn down the window.

"Telephone for you, Eric," he shouts.

For me? Maybe it's Hazel. But she never calls this early. I run inside and pick up the phone.

"Hello. Hazel?"

"What do you mean, Hello Hazel?" grumbles the man's voice on the other end of the line. "What's with Hazel, Eric?"

"Who is this?"

"Just thought I'd call and let you know," he says in a voice that sounds familiar, "you can pick me up at the train station Sunday night a little before ten."

"Jim! Is it you, Jim?"

"That always happens when I call my friends," he complains. "They always keep saying 'Who's this, who's this?' It really makes me feel like I'm a part of the action."

"Man, I'm sorry, Jim." I can't help laughing. "I never heard you on the phone before. You really grumble."

"I grumble, do I? Well, I just dare you to record your voice sometime. It's not even what I'd call a mumble."

"Hey, it's good to hear you. How are you doing anyhow?"

"I'm okay," he says. "Just thought I'd come home for the holidays and see how you're doing. I called Mom a few minutes ago and she said you're working for Uncle Rufus there at his market. Sounds like you are really settling in."

"Yeah, I got a job and stuff. It'll do for the time being. Nothing exciting, you know."

"Bored?" he asks.

"Not exactly. Sometimes it's really slow and I feel pretty alienated and all that. But this week's been really terrific. Hazel's been special lately, and the youth group is all excited about putting on a little Christmas play for their program."

"You're kidding! You mean the kids from church are doing drama?"

"Well, we find out today. The ministers have a meeting tonight. But Hazel says she thinks they might approve it. They want me to help put it together."

There's a silence on the other end of the line. "You really seem to be having a good time, Eric."

"Well, it's getting better, I guess. Rufus wants me to speak at his church Sunday night."

"At Shepherd Hill?"

"Yeah, that's what he said. I've been speaking in a good many churches lately, sometimes with Eli and sometimes by myself. It's really made things a lot more exciting."

"Yes, I'm sure." There's a tone of caution in his voice. "I'm surprised it's going so well."

"I'm surprised myself," I tell him.

"And Hazel — is that for real, Eric?"

"Yeah, man, it's real enough. I'm not sure how long it'll last or anything like that. But as of the moment we're going to Dimp's place for a skating party tonight. It's really getting to be a winter wonderland around here," I say, quipping the phrase from the background music in the store.

"Yeah." He seems to be thinking it over. "Hey, is it okay if I come home for Christmas?"

"What do you mean, is it okay! Of course. I'll head straight for the train station after church Sunday night. I'll even let you drive the old flipper home if you want to. I'll be really glad to see you."

"Thanks, Eric. I must go now. Hey, I'm really glad you're making it around there. Keep up the good work."

"I'm dying to talk to you, man."

Rufus comes rushing by just as I hang up. I haven't seen him in days.

"Still coming Sunday night?" he asks, his after shave flooding my nostrils and making me self-conscious.

"If I'm still invited," I answer.

"Of course you are. We're going to have a super program. I'm getting a fellow to bring some other converted hippies and addicts down from New York," he confides with an air of enchantment. "It might shock a few people, but it'll be a program they'll never forget."

"Yes, I'm sure it will be," I say. Wow. So I'm supposed to be one of the performers in a curious little circus that Rufus is setting up to entertain his church Sunday night. All in the name of God, of course. Apparently Rufus thinks he has me figured out. I'm not Eric to Rufus; to him I'm really just one of those awful people who now professes the same words of faith. I'm one of those sinners who has admitted I am wrong. And Rufus wants me to come crawling into his big wealthy church on my knees and admit that the way he lives is the greatest. And not just that. He's encouraging me to tell my story so that they can all be entertained by the exciting details of the big bad world. Just like those Mennonite kids in Ohio. Only Rufus is old enough to know better. But he's worse than the kids.

It takes me a while to cool off. Hazel has helped me see why Mennonites are slow to accept outsiders. Eli has helped me understand the voice of God within me. He has explained why many of his people are more concerned with tradition than they are with the voice. And grasping all of this has been hard for me. And very frustrating sometimes. Very.

But I have never been insulted by anyone the way Rufus insults me this morning as he stands there, his hand patronizingly squeezing my shoulder as he signs me up for the circus. He's going to be showing me off to his friends, using me like a monkey at the zoo who mimics the crowd and makes them laugh. If you do this well enough, Rufus seems to be hinting, I'll throw you a few peanuts. But you must be good. If you're not, there's no more circus and no more peanuts.

I spend most of the morning trying to decide if I really want to perform for Rufus or not. I know Jim never liked his uncle, and I sure didn't like him myself at first. But I guess his smooth flattery was getting to me. I was beginning to think maybe Rufus was okay. But he gave himself away this morning.

The decision is not a simple one. Maybe I'm too

sensitive about the whole monkey business. And if I don't go Sunday night, what will that prove? Rufus and his soul-saving friends will just go on saving souls. By the truckload, just like oranges. Only they'll sort out the unique ones and put them on display in their showcase of unusual goodies.

I get tired of Carolyn's chatter in the lunchroom; so I stuff my sandwiches in my jacket and go out for a walk. The sun is bright on the snow and the wind is cold. The beautiful morning is gone.

There are several sheds behind the store, and I've never taken the time to explore any of them. Storage, I suppose. I walk past the end of the long one in the back. There rising into the cold air I see four little curls of smoke. From the metal chimneys of four old brooder houses.

I wasn't aware Rufus raised chickens back here. Only last night Wilmo showed me the tiny chicks he and Menno had put in their brooder houses on the ridge behind the garage. Innocent little things. And cute.

I walk to the window and look in. But I don't see baby chicks. Instead, I see a woman near the stove, dressing. As she drops her dress over her head, I see long black hair and a beautiful Puerto Rican face. I hear a baby crying in the corner.

I pull back, sucking in my breath sharply and glancing around to see if I've been discovered. But there's nothing but the wind on the blazing snow and the little curls of smoke. And the baby crying.

Wow. I can't believe what I've seen. Surely Rufus doesn't keep a mistress. That would be ridiculous.

But what's that woman doing in there with a baby?

I slip around the back to get another view. But an old faded curtain hangs across the narrow pane. I step gingerly through the snow, sneaking up to the next half-moon of a house. Another curtain's only partly drawn. I hear some women's voices, loud in rapid conversation in a language I don't understand. Sounds like Spanish. I lean forward, searching the tiny room for the women. There are three small children, playing on a blanket on the floor. And sitting by a little table near the door are two women, dark skinned and wearing long dresses and big white coverings on their black hair. Mennonite Puerto Ricans! But what are they doing in these brooder houses?

The field of flaming snow stretches off into the distance, forming a horizontal line of fire against the sky. I stand there, squinting and shivering and listening to the wind. There's a Latin sadness in the song it sings.

These sheds are not used for brooding chicks, that's obvious. But what is going on? A thousand thoughts go racing through my mind as I stand there in the wilderness of frozen white, the beautiful morning gone forever. And I feel like a little child who has just overheard his father telling a lie.

"I believe I might have stumbled on another zoo," I say aloud. But no one hears. The baby goes on crying and the women go on talking. But the wind never listens. And my voice is lost in the wilderness.

I duck past the window and peep into the fourth brooder house. Another dwelling. There's an old rug by the door and a cot in the corner where the ceiling meets the floor. Several utensils hang along the wall above the shelf of food. There's no refrigerator, no washbowl, no cupboards. It's like a home without a house.

There's a fifth shack, but it's empty. There's a calendar on the wall and a few old bent wires for hanging clothes. The place looks cold as death.

I lose all sense of time as I wander among the shacks in the snow, trying to discover what it's all about. My toes are freezing and I seek shelter in the big shed that hides the shacks from the rest of the world. It's dark inside. But I see another door. There is a stairway leading into the cellar.

I'm halfway down the steps when I hear someone laughing. It's a loud, hearty laugh. I stoop down and look around. There's a light at the far end of the cellar, coming through an open doorway. And the laughing comes from the same direction.

I grope among the crates of celery and the mounds of potatoes, moving slowly toward the light. There are several laughing now. Several men.

I stop in the shadow by the doorway. At first all I see is piles of celery on a table. Then I see some feet standing in the puddle of water that surrounds the table. There's the sound of running water and the chop-chop of knives. The place is very cold.

Then someone begins to sing, in a rich Spanish-sounding voice. I never do see the singer's face. I close my eyes and turn away, a numb emptiness boring a hollow hole in my heart.

Once many years ago I stumbled into a little slum

on the back side of a dump in southern Tennessee. But I was younger then. I remember being more curious than angry as I wandered among the shacks in that dump, taking pictures and talking to the children. But that was long ago. I'm older now, and a slum is no longer a place for cameras. It's a place for disease and coffins and unheard songs of death. Not cameras.

Stanley comes rushing up to me when I get back to the store. "Where have you been, Eric? I was looking for you. Tim needs help with the meats."

I stare at him. "Say, Stanley, did Rufus ever think of hiring Spanish people to work for him?"

"You mean, Puerto Ricans? Sure, he hires lots of them. Not so many over winter, of course. They hate the cold. But in the summer they come by the dozens."

"That should be a big help," I say, hoping he'll tell me more.

"Oh, sure. They work real cheap, you know," he smiles. "If it wouldn't be for them, we'd never be able to run such a big operation. We couldn't possibly get the local help to work in the fields with the produce the way those Puerto Rican boys do. And, of course, our own people would want better wages. And rightly so. Only that would run us out of business in less than a year." His tone becomes more confidential. "Those dirty rascals are always giving us trouble, though. If it's not more money they want, it's longer weekends. But you know how they drink. So Rufus refuses to give them Saturdays off. They'd just get drunk."

He looks toward the back of the store in the direction of the big sheds. "Rufus got a Spanish evangelist in here last summer and that really changed things. A lot of them were converted and they don't give us trouble anymore. Rufus even helped them start their own church down along Rabbit Lake."

"Do they live in town?" I ask him.

"In town!" he exclaims. "Are you kidding? Where would they live? Who's going to let them ruin their neighborhood? No, Rufus had some brooder houses fixed up for them. But some of them don't keep up with their rent. It's a real pain."

I can't believe my ears. "Did you say rent?"

"Yeah, it's only forty-five bucks a month. But I have to collect it, and that's one of my worst jobs. I had to throw one of them out several weeks ago because he couldn't pay his rent. I really hated to do it, but you can't just go on giving people the benefit of the doubt forever. Especially not that kind of people."

"Well, they certainly get more than forty-five bucks a month, don't they?" I ask in a tone that's remarkably calm.

"Forty-five?" Stanley looks at me. "Oh, sure, over twice that much. I can never figure out what they do with it all." He turns and hurries away, leaving me angry and cold, my fingers digging holes in the uneaten sandwiches in my pocket.

11

Hazel skates well. She skims effortlessly along the ice, lifting her skates in smooth rhythm, her long scarf snug about her face in the crisp cold. The pond fills a greater part of the meadow below Dimp's house and the skaters have come by the dozens. Dimp has the lower end of the pond blocked off for the youth group.

I'm not so hot on ice. I've tried it only twice before and Wilmo's skates are a size too large. So I wobble a lot. And fall. My pants are half wet before the party even begins. Hazel gets tired of my falling all the time and skates off to join a game of "crack the whip." I don't blame her, really. But I am disappointed. And after another series of falls, I drag myself over to the fire to warm up and dry off.

"Crack the whip" takes up a major part of the evening. The skaters rush down the ice in a long line, shouting and laughing amid the contented rumble of the ice. Then those at one end suddenly stop abruptly and swing the whole line around in a circle. The speed on the other end is terrific. Often the line breaks because the skaters can't hold on to each other as they go spinning across the pond like a spoke in a great big wheel of ice.

I watch them, wishing I could join the fun. But it doesn't really matter. My heart is far away. I keep seeing those five shacks in the snow, their little curls of smoke rising noiselessly into the cold. And I keep seeing the smirk on Stanley's face. It makes me sick.

Sara comes up and sits beside me at the fire. She wears slacks under her dress. It looks sort of corny.

"That the new fad?" I ask her with a grin.

"What?"

"Well, I never saw anyone wear slacks under a dress before. Is it a new thing?" I notice she's the only girl wearing slacks.

"Yeah, I guess." The light of the fire dances across her hesitant smile. "You like it, Eric?"

"Sure. I'm not really big on fashions."

"I'm not either. I'm just trying to be sensible. It's almost down to zero and I don't see why a girl should go skating around with her legs exposed in this type of weather. I don't care if the others like it or not."

We sit by the fire and listen to the rumble of the ice and the frolic of the skaters. Sara hums to herself and throws little snowballs into the fire. There's a happy freedom in her big face.

"Do you know where Rabbit Lake is?" I ask her.

"Sure, it's about four miles from here," she says.

"Is it a town?"

"No, it's a big lake. And in the summer the Puerto Ricans live out there in cabins. But no one's there in winter. Except their church. It's an old building the government used to use, but they built a new place on the other end of the lake. So the Puerto Ricans use it as a church."

108

"How come they don't come to your church, Sara?"

"Oh, they don't want to," she says. "We do let them use our basement sometimes. Eli knows a lot of them." She goes back to throwing snowballs into the fire and humming her tune. "You ought to go out there sometime," she says after a bit. "It's like a haunted village in the winter. It really scares me at night. We often stop there when we're out having fun."

I watch her as she talks. I want to touch her eyes and help her see. But she's lost in a world of her own with problems thick and heavy. Life is hard enough for Sara. So I hold my tongue and watch the fire.

She gets up to go. "Come on, Eric," she says, "aren't you going to skate anymore?"

"I'm not so hot at it, Sara."

"Come on, I'll help you," she says, pulling me to my feet. She looks at my skates. "Oh, goodness, your skates are too wobbly. Sit down, I'll show you how to tighten them."

I watch her as she works at the laces, pulling them tight and holding them with her thumb while she ties them firmly. "There you are, Eric," she looks up, smiling. "That'll give you better support."

She helps me learn to step corners. It takes a lot of patience. I'm just not athletic. But Sara makes it a lot of fun.

As we go back to join the others at the fire, Sara takes my arm. "May I ask you something, Eric?"

"Sure, Sara."

"Do you think I might get a part in the play?"

she asks. Her eyes can't hide her strong curiosity.

"Would you like a part?"

"I'd give anything for it. I was never allowed to do anything in school. My father was against it."

"I'm not sure who's going to make the decisions about the casting," I tell her. "It's not been approved yet, you know. And, of course, if it is, we don't have time to do too big a piece. Christmas will soon be here. But I think you should get a part. I believe you'll do a good job."

Her eyes light up. "Thanks," she says. "I understand that things aren't definite yet. But thanks anyhow."

Dimp and his sister are serving the skaters cookies and hot chocolate as they mill around the fire, drinking, chewing, and talking. "Come on, Eric," he calls, waving a cup in my direction. "It's not going to get any hotter."

The kids are friendly. "Hey, man, you ought to help crack the whip," Lonnie Groff says to me. "We missed you out there."

"I would love to if I knew how to skate."

Hazel comes skating up. "But you could help clean off the ice," she says real loud. Everyone laughs and I can feel myself getting red, my face trying to smile and stay calm at the same moment.

"I'm good at that," I admit.

"We're all good at that," Lonnie chuckles.

Mel, Jr., launches into another story about their milkman and the moment passes. But something in me is hurt. Hazel was deliberately making fun of me.

I watch her over by the fire, talking to two guys

110

about my age. They laugh a lot. Then they go speeding off across the ice, the three of them graceful as birds in the sky. I watch them disappear into the crowd in the other corner of the pond.

"It's enough to make you mad," says Mel, Jr. "If he's not slipping on the manure, he's slipping on the ice. Dumb milkman."

It's almost ten o'clock before I see Hazel again. She's sitting on a stump near the bank, talking to the same two guys. The one in the blue cap is telling a story about school when I come sliding to a stop. My skate blade catches a stick and it sends me sprawling face down across the cold, wet ice.

They giggle. I collect myself, but not before Hazel blurts out, "That's what I call a good clean job of it."

The boys giggle some more. The blue cap helps me up. "It just doesn't work to try to skate on those sticks," he says. I glare at him.

"Fellows, I'd like you to meet Eric," Hazel says. "He's visiting in the neighborhood. Eric, this is Marv and Merv."

"Hi," they chorus together.

But I don't say a word. I just stand there, cold and wet on my wobbly skates, trying to understand why Hazel has become so nasty. But she avoids my eyes.

"I'm going home, Hazel," I say in my low voice, hoping she'll come to her senses.

"Oh, that's too bad," she responds. "I hope you enjoyed your visit."

"I don't know what kind game you're playing,

111

Hazel. But I don't think it's very funny."

"Who's laughing?"

Our eyes lock across the fire in a strange sort of battle of wits. But she doesn't give. There's a faint smile playing around her mouth and there's a teasing twinkle in her eyes. But she doesn't give an inch.

"I suppose you can find another way home." I say, dropping my eyes and brushing the snowy ice off my pants.

"Oh, sure, Eric. Sara can drop me off."

As I climb the bank, the skates in my hands, feet numb and eyes watering, I turn to see if Hazel might be watching. But she's having a great time with Merv and Marv, and she never notices.

I stop at Hazel's place anyhow, to see if Eli's home from the meeting yet. He walks from the barn as I pull up to the gate.

"Hello, Eric. Have a nice evening?"

"No, I didn't, quite frankly. Did you?"

That slow smile spreads across the prophet's face. "I admire your frankness, Eric." He pauses, reaching through the car window to lay a gentle hand on my arm.

"No dice, right?" I can see he's trying to break the news.

"What?"

"You didn't approve the play, did you?" But I don't wait for his answer. I can see it in his face. I shift the old flipper into low and let the clutch fly. I can hear the stones grinding under the tires as I roar around the barn and back on the road. And I never leave my foot off the pedal until I skid to a stop back at Jim's place, my teeth gritted and my eyes narrowed the way they get when I'm very angry.

I sit there in the cold car a long time, trying to put it all together. But it doesn't go together. Obviously, I'm never going to belong to these people. They're so slow to accept new people and new ideas. Why did I ever expect them to? Why did I ever stay here in the first place? They're no different from other people. It's just the way Hazel said. People are people, the world around.

It begins to snow again and I watch the heavy flakes pellet toward the ground, driven by the wind and overanxious to reach the cold earth. What a disappointment each flake must experience when it smacks against the frozen ground! So this is it? This is what it's all about.

The numbness leaves my feet tingling and burning and moves to my heart. It stays there for many years.

Decades later I drag myself to the house. It's a long walk up to the porch. It's as though my whole life is laid before me and I live each moment again. And when I reach the porch, I lift my eyes to peer through the storm, off to the hills behind the house. "O God, from where is my help going to come?" But my cry is lost in the night.

When I waken, my head is hot and my throat sore. I can hear Anna in the kitchen and the men at the barn. But before I can reach for my clock, its shrill alarm shatters the stillness. I smack the button down and climb out. To face another day. Among a strange people.

Thursday comes and goes and Friday follows. Stanley asks me to work overtime on Saturday and it's almost nine o'clock that night before I sit down to work on my speech for Shepherd Hill.

I drive to church by myself Sunday morning and leave immediately after the benediction, before Eli can even get to the back to shake my hand. I want to think. Alone. So I drive around the countryside all afternoon, trying to focus my thoughts for Shepherd Hill and the big circus.

The church is packed when I get there. The organist is playing so loud I can't even hear the lady up front singing as she leads the congregation in "Joy to the World." People are sitting in the aisles and standing along the walls. The usher tries to send me to the basement but I tell him I'm supposed to be in the program. So he lets me sneak in the back.

Rufus gets up when the organ stops and the lady sits down. As usual he wears a gay shirt and a bright blue double-breasted suit. With a flashy smile, he clears his throat, and the circus is under way.

The people sit up attentively as he introduces the first addict of the evening. And they never miss a move as the big fellow strides up on the pulpit and yanks up his sleeve.

"See that?" he demands in a loud clownish voice. "Those marks were put there by a needle. The needle of Satan. But by the help of God, I've kicked that old devil good-bye." He laughs, and they laugh.

Then he launches into a long yarn about his past life, the times he almost got killed, the jobs he pulled,

114

and the fights he had with the cops. The audience is spellbound, licking it up like a child tasting honey for the first time.

The second "convert" is even more dramatic, jumping around the pulpit and topping off his performance with a little song and dance. The audience laughs repeatedly, sitting on the edge of their benches and wishing Rufus would plan the program more often.

The third speaker is a girl, billed as both a converted hippie and a converted addict. And she really lays it on them. The men especially enjoy her routine. And I have to admit, she can really tell it like it is.

It's already late when Rufus gets around to introducing me. "I'm happy to say I have a personal involvement with Eric and his new faith," he says. Baloney.

I know that as a circus progresses, each act must outdo the previous ones. So the audience is expecting a big finale. Too bad.

I decide not to use the pulpit. I walk to the lower podium and snap on the mike. Then I stand there for an endless moment, just looking at the audience.

"I have only one question to ask you tonight," I say in a voice that is quiet and calm. "Why do we build so many cages?"

It gets so silent in that big auditorium that I declare I can hear the wind in the trees outside the church. There's a human sadness in the silence, the kind you hear in the quiet of a big circus tent after the crowd has laughed themselves sick and everyone has gone home. And you can hear that same wind in the trees outside the big empty tent. Only the crowd is still here.

"Why are we always putting each other in cages?" I ask them as I go on. "Why can't we learn that this is what Christmas is all about — no more prison, no more slavery, no more circus, no more cages?

"Many of you here tonight dress the way you do and live the way you do and vacation the way you do because you resent having grown up in a cage where everyone was always looking at you and laughing at you. You got tired of being different. So you jumped into another cage, a larger cage, where people don't gawk and laugh and think you're odd. Only, you're not free. It's just a bigger cage. But you don't know it."

It's one of my inspired moments and I feel the voice within me crying out. "My friends, in the name of God, why? Why do we push people into more cages and more cages, putting them on exhibit and using them to make a quick dollar while they entertain our friends? And then we call it church. Whether it's conservative Amish or Mennonites, or whether it's Puerto Ricans, or whether it's drug addicts or so-called hippies — my friends, it's wrong. That's what I've learned, living here among you."

The people sit frozen on their benches. "The message of Christmas," I say in a whisper of the voice within me, "is peace, and freedom, and love and goodwill. My brothers and sisters, let us not build any more cages. And let's find the keys to the prisons we have already so selfishly built. And let's open the doors and throw away the keys and praise God."

I slip out the front door, leaving them alone in the big crowded church. I start the old flipper and head for the train station. The organ is playing "Silent Night" as I leave the churchyard.

Jim is waiting for me on the platform. I jump out and help him with his luggage. Without a word. He takes my hand and shakes it long and hard. Without a word. The station is cold and empty and we stand there, alone, in the night, like strangers meeting friends.

"Merry Christmas," he says. "It's good to be home."

12

Clerks usually don't have heavy black eyebrows. Especially not in the radio department of a men's store. But this guy's got whoppers.

"It's a disgrace," I tell Jim.

He smiles. "Maybe the kid's got a problem."

"What do you mean — maybe?" I ask him. "It looks pretty obvious to me."

And the poor fellow's problem is rather obvious. Only it isn't hair that bothers him. It's questions.

"What's the difference between these two transistors?" the lady with the floppy hat is asking the clerk.

"I'll check," he says nervously.

Another woman grabs his arm. "Hey, boy, I was in here last week and you gave me the wrong plug."

"I gave you the wrong plug, the way it looks, lady."

"Listen, boy, don't you go around repeating me," she storms. "I want to know which plug I need. And I'm in a hurry. My parking meter just ran out."

"I'll check," says Eyebrows. "I'm sorry about both your plug and your meter."

As he turns toward the counter, he bumps into a freckled youngster holding a crumpled twenty-dollar bill in his hand. "Which of the clock radios have luminous hands?" he asks.

"I'll check."

"I like to see it at night," the youngster says.

The clerk is getting a little upright. "All right, all right," he raises his voice, shaking his eyebrows and pushing them into a dark frown, "I said I'll check."

Several checkings later Jim gets in a word about the radio he and I are buying for his parents for Christmas. At first Jim didn't like the idea because he was scared they might be offended. "I'd hate to spend all that money and then have them upset about it," he said. But this morning he got up suggesting we come to town to see what they have.

We settle on an AM-FM set in a conservative dark green. "Mom likes green a lot," Jim says.

The town is full of shoppers, rushing in and out of the stores with more scurry than usual, carrying packages of many colors. Jim knows a lot of people and stops to chat with several. He listens mostly. And there's an uneasy self-consciousness in his face as he listens to their talk. His smile is slow, and he seldom laughs. There's a sadness about him, and the people sense it and try to comfort him. But the last of the Witmers must face it by himself. So he just nods and smiles faintly and pulls himself away.

"People can really make you tired," he says as we kick the snow from our shoes and jump into the car. He sits hunched over the steering wheel, his eyes watching the stores. "They say such empty things," he says.

119

On the way back to the farm we pass through the town that left its decorations up all summer. And just as Wilmo predicted, there's not a star in sight. Even the bushes on the square are bare.

Back at the farm we sneak in the back door and hide the radio in a closet in the attic. A hockey stick falls out at us as Jim opens the door of the dusty nook. He stoops and lifts it slowly, running his hands along its smooth edge. "John was good on ice," he says.

He shows me other things. A bookcase they built together for a contest in shop. An express wagon. "We used to pretend it was a cattle truck," Jim says. "Simon broke it riding backwards down the back lane one day. It was really nuts. But it sure looked funny."

There's an old birdhouse, a real mansion, paint peeling now and roof partly broken. And there's an old saddle. "Pop got tired of always having to coax us to go after the cows at milking time. So he promised to buy us a pony if we'd promise to fetch the cows." He smiles in the shadows of the old attic. "We called him Conrad. We must have ridden the old fellow to death, though. He died the first Christmas we had him. Pop was pretty upset." Jim runs his palm across the leather, his eyes watching it the way you watch a cloud at night.

It's the type of scene symbolic writers spend their lives trying to construct. But there's nothing to construct here. Jim and I sit alone in the shallow light of the big attic, fragments from the past strewn all about us. Fragments of lives, fragments of dreams.

Once upon a happy time. Now gone. And only the musty sentimentality of echoes, muffled by many winters of dust and forgetting, to make the attic come alive.

After dinner we wash the old flipper and help Menno and Wilmo with the weekend chores. We lean on the cow stable doors and watch the snow. "Home is a strange thing," Jim says. "Is it where your memories live — or is it where you yourself live?"

I spit the way Wilmo does. "I think home is a place you never find. At least that's how it is for me."

"Every time I come here I feel like I belong less."

"That's because your heart is other places."

"But it's here," Jim answers with a sad tremor in his voice. "If home were out there in those other places, how come we brought John home here to bury him when he hadn't been home for two years? No one around here had any idea what he was angry and concerned about. No one even understood the world he lived in. None of them understood the meaning of his death. But we brought him here and buried him on the hill, beside Simon."

"Who else would have buried him?"

The answer is never spoken. That's the way life is, I guess. So we just stand there, leaning on the door and watching the creek wind its way down through the snowy meadow, streaming toward the ocean far away.

"John is sort of a hero around the university these days," Jim says. "Things are quiet now, but I often see his name scrawled on the walls of buildings. 'Remember Big John' it says. I even saw his name

121

on the big statue of freedom in front of the library. It makes me really feel funny. It's like he's more alive now than he was before he was killed."

"But no one cared enough to come and help bury him."

Jim looks at me. "No one but you, Eric. And for that I'll be forever thankful."

We watch the creek again. The sun has gone away and the air is heavy with snow.

"I suppose I was really foolish to stay here, Jim," I say.

"Why do you say that?"

"Because I should have known I could never be accepted by your people. Even though they've been quite friendly, probably more so than a lot of other ethnic groups."

"But, Eric, you do belong more than you think. Since I'm home this week I've heard dozens of people tell me how much they appreciate you." He chuckles as he continues. "Honestly, it made me sort of jealous. I began to think you belonged here more than me."

The irony of it all makes me chuckle too. "But I wasn't born here, Jim, and that makes all the difference."

"But you told me this is a place of birth for you. I never forgot that, Eric. The whole way back to the city I kept hearing you say that."

I smile at him. "Home is where you're born, I guess. Only I wasn't as born as I thought I was."

We talk till milking time. I tell him all about Hazel and Eli and Rufus and the circus at Shepherd Hill.

And he listens the way he listened to the people in town, nodding and spitting and smiling now and then. And once again I realize we're almost brothers, the two of us. Almost brothers, but strangers nonetheless.

We do the milking early so that we won't be late for the Christmas program. Lonnie Groff had asked me to read a poem but I told him I'd rather not. I had offered my services in helping with the play, and the ministers turned me down. So let them do their own program. I didn't want anything to do with it. In fact, I wouldn't even go tonight if Jim didn't want to so much. "It was always one of my favorite things," he says. "It was the highlight of Christmas."

The five of us crowd into Menno's black Chevy and head for the fire hall where we park among the other black cars. It is snowing as we step from the car and follow the others into the building. At the door I take Jim's arm and pull him aside.

"Let's sit near the back," I whisper, "if you don't mind. I'm sort of embarrassed."

But the back two rows are already filled with young people from church. So we slip in the end of the third row, beside Noah Dombach and two of his boys.

In the city, Christmas was always a mixture of hustle and music and parties. Last year a friend and I spent the whole vacation with some girls he knew in the Village. Much more fun than the boredom of going home to my mother and her fancy world of make-believe.

But here in this fire hall tonight, there's no make-believe. The kids sing in candlelight. And it's not that the candlelight's so special. It's the way they sing.

Their faces are rosy, open, happy. The parents sit back and smile and sing along from time to time. It's as though they understand Christmas. And they are glad.

Hazel stands near the edge of the group, as they sing. She is simply stunning in a new dress of dark, deep red. The flickering light dances in her face and fills it with tender innocence. And my heart quickens. It's been days since we've spoken. I never wanted to see her again. But I've never seen her more attractive, never more irresistible. It's as though you'd think she could never utter an unkind word, lovely angel that she seems. I want to touch her and hear her laugh and listen to her speak of life and living. But it's not that simple. And she knows it too.

The music fills the room with joy, its fire igniting little lights from face to face. It's one of those perfect moments and I find myself forgetting all my grudges as I listen to the songs that sweep across the audience, row on row. Sara reads a poem toward the end, and does it very well. It touches the people's hearts. Noah blows his nose to keep from crying and his boys sit front and drink in every word. But Sara keeps on going, giving each word its special tone, her face full of fire and her voice full of flame. Even some of the kids wipe their eyes.

One of the older ministers gets up when all the readings and singings are done. I suppose he's one of those who vetoed the play and for a while it makes me mad. But then his voice pierces my anger and I hear his words.

"God came down to man on Christmas," he says in

his dry voice with the nasal accent. "That's a miracle. And I don't want anyone asking why or how or when. God visited us and brought us hope and forgiveness. And that's all that matters. That's the good news."

I'm still thinking it over when the youth sing their last song and the house lights come on. God became man. Wow. Of course I knew that's what it was all about — but he said it so simply. Not as an idea, not as a piece of history. He said it, uninteresting as his manner was, as though it was exciting good news. As though it changed the world. And he believed it. And no one asked why or how or when. They too believed. And were glad.

Jim is shaking hands as I turn to go. So I shake too. The two young fellows behind me look familiar but somehow I can't remember where I saw them before.

"Good evening," I say, extending my hand. "I don't know if I've met you before or not. I'm Eric."

"I'm Marv," the first one says, pumping my hand up and down so hard it hurts my fingers. "And this is my twin Merv. We're cousins of Hazel's."

I don't know if my face gets red or not but I surely feel red. "Oh, yeah," I say, "I met you at the skating party last week. I didn't know you without your cap."

They giggle a bit. "We come here every Christmas," Merv says. "Our folks are missionaries in Africa."

"It's been nice meeting you," I say.

"Same here," chirps Marv. "Maybe we'll see you

again next Christmas. Hazel says you and she got something going." They titter again and I'm sure my face is red now. I smile awkwardly, and turn to go. "Maybe," I say.

Sara comes rushing up to me when I get to the back. "Did you like it?" she asks, her big face hanging on my answer.

"It was well done, Sara. The people were touched."

"But you didn't like it?"

"I liked the whole program very much, Sara. Especially your poem."

"Lonnie was upset that you wouldn't do it," she says, eyes serious and confidential. "And I was upset, too."

"But why?"

"Because you could have done it so well, Eric."

"Sara, you were terrific. I couldn't have done half as well."

"That's not true, and I'm disappointed." She glances around and then narrows her eyes as she continues. "I was over there at Shepherd Hill last Sunday, Eric, and I have never been so touched as I was by your testimony. It was like you were some sort of prophet."

Prophet! I almost laugh in her face but her eyes hold my laughter. "God could have used you here tonight, too." She turns and walks away, the sting of her words still in my face. I stand there dazed, watching her disappear in the crowd, and realize that she was hurt and disappointed. And I thought nobody cared.

Hazel is waiting for me in the snow outside the door. Her smile is hesitant, her voice almost timid.

"I'm really sorry about the play, Eric," she says. "I honestly thought they'd approve it."

"That's okay," I say. "I enjoyed your program a great deal."

"Thanks." The snowflakes fall gently on her dark hair, and her lips are as red as her dress. She is a lovely woman, and in the shadows she is lovelier than ever. Her eyes reach out to touch mine, to make peace, to seek kindness and trust.

"I love you, Hazel," I whisper. "I love you and hate you and love you some more."

She takes in my love with love of her own. And for a moment we are true, our lives open, embracing each other, and pure.

It's a long time before she moves. Her face is glowing, her voice bursting with warmth. "That was a beautiful thing to say," she murmurs. "If only we can turn the hate into love, all will be well."

The snow falls between us, the night wind soft as our whispers of love. And deep in my soul I know that our love is just like the snow, fragile and beautiful and soft. And when the day comes, it will melt and disappear into the earth.

But the snow falls between us and the day is far away. Tonight.

13

Christmas Day on the farm. No tree, no fancy lights, no Santa, no stocking by no big roaring fireplace. Just oatmeal. Oatmeal and lots of other food. And digging out from a snowstorm.

The alarm goes off a half hour early, rousing us to the day of celebration. Jim grunts and I grunt back. Anna's having all her brothers and sisters for a big feast today. And Jim and I have been signed up as waiters.

Wilmo sticks his head in our door, his eyes as large as his bald spot. "It's a real blizzard!" he exclaims in his groggy voice.

"What!"

"Come on, get out of bed, you lazy bums," he says, tugging at his baggy pajamas. "We'll have to open the lane so the company can get here."

"I guess that's your job, Wilmo," Jim yawns, still in bed. "We'll help with the milking and we'll help Mother. But the lane — that's your assignment."

The hired man, still clutching his rumpled flannels, marches his bare feet over to the bed and jerks the covers off, leaving the pajamaless Jim hugging his bare legs as the cold air rushes in. "Now you listen to me, James Witmer," Wilmo says. "You're not getting out of any work today." Jim laughs at him.

Menno, fully dressed, stands in the doorway watching. "Boys," he says, including all three of us in the same word. "Boys, let's get to the barn. Wilmer, get dressed."

The hired man obeys the farmer, but not before he gives Jim a meaningful look. "No tricks," he warns.

"Better get some clothes on," Jim tells him. "Don't worry about me, Wilmo. I can work twice as fast as you."

"Oh, sure, if you feel like it," Wilmo answers crossly. "Only most of the time you don't feel like it." The two of them keep at it the whole way through the milking. Wilmo acts mad, but he enjoys it as much as Jim.

After a breakfast of hot steaming oatmeal and some "mush-an'-puddins" on toast smeared thick with apple butter and onions, we hurry to the barn to put the snowplow on the tractor while Menno finishes up in the milk house. Jim and I drag out some heavy chains for the back wheels and Wilmo fixes a broken piece of the "heat-houser." It takes a lot of grunting in three-part harmony to get the chains on tight. Then Jim drives into the plow and we fasten it securely. We throw some wheel weights on the back hitch to offset the plow a bit. Jim races the engine and fills the tank with gas. Then we roll open the door and Jim lets the clutch fly. Wow. What an impact! The big tractor charges into the sprawling snowdrift outside the door and sends it spraying the whole way down the barn hill.

I sweep off the porch and shovel the walks while

Jim and Wilmo plow the lane. The wind blows the snow across the fields in a fine mist that leaves new little driftlets where the tractor has just plowed.

It's almost ten-thirty when we get to the house. The smell of turkey and cranberries and corn and a hundred other foods rushes out to meet us as we come in, half frozen, snow heavy about our coats and washing our faces. Jim's parents are working by the stove, lifting big heavy kettles and stirring the feast. It's the first time I've seen Menno in an apron. One of Anna's, the kind with a bib up the front that loops around the neck.

"This is real Christmas," Jim says. "Lots of snow, lots of food and relatives, and Pop in an apron. And gifts."

"Gifts?" I ask, pulling off my boots.

He grins. "You don't have to have a tree to have gifts, Eric."

It's a truly joyous time, the happiest I have with the Witmers during my short visit. Menno carries in a carton from the back room, a mischievous smile on his face. Wilmo, face scrubbed and hair slicked back, sneaks in with a shopping bag of his own. Jim scurries around the kitchen, hiding his packages, and stuffs several envelopes in his shirt pocket. And I arrive at the party with my carefully chosen and carefully wrapped gifts, a little emotional and uptight about telling them thank you and good-bye.

Anna breaks the suspense. "Pop," she says, "I want you to leave the room for about five minutes."

Menno acts startled. "Me — leave the room? What's going on here?"

"Now you just listen on me, Pop," his wife says, giving him a playful push toward the stairs. It's the most I ever see them touch each other.

Menno goes up the stairs and closes the door. Anna watches him and sees him open the door a crack to take a peep. "Menno, now you quit that," the farmer's wife calls. Then she turns to Jim. "Can you and Wilmer handle it?"

"Sure, Mom," he says.

"What is it, Anna?" Wilmo asks.

"Just go with Jim."

They go down to the cellar and Anna stands watch on the stairs, making sure her husband doesn't cheat. There's a special excitement in the air which seems foreign to this kitchen as I've experienced it these few weeks since that cold train brought us here to bury Big John. The stern, almost brutal seriousness that dominates the conversations and the silence in this house has suddenly brightened into gaiety, happy secrets, and surprise. I'm glad I didn't miss Christmas with these people.

Jim and Wilmo come stumbling up the steps with an oldish-looking rocking chair, newly refinished. Anna pulls a large knitted afghan from a brown paper bag and lays it on the rocker seat and up over the back. Then she steps back and looks at it. It's quite handsome in the bright morning sun.

"Boy, oh, boy," Wilmo whispers, "is that for him?"

Anna nods. "Like it?"

It's Wilmo's turn to nod. "Wish I had one," he says.

"Okay, Pop, you can come down now."

Menno opens the door and comes down the steps

with a grin. "I hope it's not a disappointment," he says, trying to act unimpressed by the fuss. But he can't hide his delight when he sees the rocker. "My, my, my," he says. "Who's that for, Mom?"

She answers with a smile. "Come on, sit in it," she urges him.

He sits. He rocks. He smiles.

"My, my, my," he purrs in that small voice of his.

"Pop Metzler picked it up at a sale," Anna says.

"And she made the afghan," Wilmo adds.

Menno just keeps smiling. "I like it, Mom," he says, rocking back and forth and burying the back of his bald head in the afghan. "Makes me sleepy."

The gifts are mostly practical. Wilmo gets a new shirt, a pair of suspenders, and a new cap with ear muffs. He gives Anna an apron and Menno some new rubbers. And he gives me a pocketknife. Five blades and a can opener.

Jim gets some clothes from his parents, a book about worldliness, and ten dollars. Menno gives his wife a new pitcher for the breakfast table to make up for the one he'd accidentally broken several weeks ago.

Jim gives everyone an envelope with a riddle telling where to find their gifts. It's a real scramble. "John and I used to do it," he says. My yellow and blue package contains a book of Shelley's poems and Simon and Garfunkel's most recent album. And a beret. A black beret. "It was John's," he says. "He'd want you to have it."

I hold it in my hand and I feel my legs trembling. A shirt from his parents, a knife from Wilmo, and a black beret from the twins. The beret that everyone knew, the symbol of the Revolution, the mantle of him who lies buried on the hill. Mine. "I can't take it, Jim."

His eyes are gentle in the light of Christmas Day. "There's no one else who can take it, Eric. You're the only real friend he had. You're the only one who stood by him in death." His tone is firm. "Please accept it."

I can feel the tears in my eyes. "It's one of the nicest things you could have done, Jim." I can see the tears now as they brim my lids. "Thanks," I whisper.

We stand there, shaking hands and fighting our tears, alone together while the others hunt their gifts and open them around the table, unaware that the past has come home for Christmas. There's something final about it, something that has passed forever from us as I finger the soft black cloth of the beret. Big John is dead. He won't be coming back to claim his mantle. And Jim knows it.

The moment passes. And now I know that I must go. I think I first knew that I was leaving that night after the skating party when Eli tried to break the news of the veto to me. I saw then that this was not my home. These people would never trust me enough to make me theirs. At least not for many years. And by then they may be as corrupted by the modern world as Rufus is.

The beret is like a silent call that beckons me back to the action, back to the real world. And I must go. A different person. Different indeed. Alone and troubled and a wee bit happier. A wee bit more sad.

The radio is a surprise. Menno lifts it out of its box and sets it on the table in front of his wife. She touches it. "What is it, Jim?" she asks.

"That's a radio, Anna," Wilmo pipes up.

"A radio." I can't tell if she likes it or not.

"That's a pretty expensive gift," the farmer says, looking at his son.

"I like the color," his mother admits, rubbing her fingers across its smooth surface. "Thank you, boys."

"Plug it in, or we'll never know if it works," Wilmo says, unwinding the cord.

"Not now, Wilmer," Mrs. Witmer says. "We better get ready for the company. Let's clean the table and get out the extra boards."

As we pull the table open and put in the extra boards, I turn to Jim. "Did they like it?"

"I think so," he says. "They didn't want to act too excited. But I think they'll keep it."

Wilmo bumps me with the new toolbox I gave him. "You give nice gifts," he says.

The uncles and aunts and cousins pour in by the dozens. "Forty-three in all," Anna tells me. "Of course, maybe Rufus and his family won't come."

The men lounge about the living room, shaking hands, kidding each other, patting hungry stomachs, and telling stories about the snowstorm. Uncle Willis comes up with the best tales, and as they wait for dinner, time and again Uncle Willis has them laughing uncontrollably. One of Uncle Norman's boys has a good bit of trouble sobering up. Norman gives him the eye. "That'll make him brace up," Jim whispers. "When Norman gives you the eye, you know you're not facing the happiest moment of your life. His cows even hate him." But Willis's next joke has the poor boy rolling off his chair again. This time Norman gives Willis the eye, but Willis ignores his brother's glare.

Jim and I hang around the kitchen, trying to be of help to his mother. The aunts talk a lot. Seems as though at least three or four conversations are buzzing all the time.

Jim chats with several of the girls. One cousin is especially attractive, and Jim introduces her to me. Her name is Barbara. She attends a Mennonite college in another state.

"It's much better than last year," she tells Jim. "We have a new professor in charge of the department."

"What are you studying, Barbara?" I ask.

"Nursing."

"That's a good old Mennonite standby," Jim says. "I think if we'd take all the people in medicine and sociology out of the Mennonite Church, the whole thing would go up in smoke."

Barbara agrees. "But I'm not in nursing just because it's popular," she insists. "I really feel that's where the Lord wants me."

Rufus arrives just as the uncles and their sons are getting up to come to the table. He smiles at everyone but there's no handshaking. Louise is dressed in her usual red. Their children and the other children watch each other uncomfortably. "Many of them never see each other except at Christmas," Jim says.

135

The adults eat in the kitchen and the children eat at two tables in the side room. Grandpa Metzler says "grace." Then the dishes begin to make their rounds, and the feast is under way.

As I move from room to room, refilling dishes and platters and water glasses, I keep remembering the first day I saw these people. There was no feast that day. They had all trooped into the front room, heavy with the burden of death, troubled with the terrible task of burying a son, a twin, a wearer of the black beret. The faces, happy and festive today, had been cold and solemn behind their wire glasses that day long ago when the leaves were falling on the hill. Leaves already brown with death. Now, like the grass, buried beneath the snow.

Perhaps the grass in that little cemetery under the trees will come alive again someday. Perhaps the snow will melt away and the sun will call forth new grass to green the ground. Perhaps. But as I move from plate to plate today, serving the feast, watching the faces, and listening to the laughter of these people, a painful sadness fills my soul. For a moment this morning, when Jim and I were all alone together, alone and unprepared, the past came back to visit us and say good-bye. We hardly heard it in the silence. And as it turned to bid farewell, wrapping its pale cape tighter about the memories it carried, it whispered something too soft to hear. Something about a new greenness, a new happiness. Something about tomorrow. But neither of us heard. And then it was gone.

Later, when the relatives are leaving, I stand by the kitchen window, watching the hill, hoping for some last word from those trees, some last understanding. But the words never come.

Rufus finds me and stands beside me, looking up across the landscape. It's the first time I've known him to be quiet and speechless. Perhaps he understands more than I think he does.

"To some the snow is cold," he says. "To some it is clean. To others it is beautiful. And to still others it is only something that melts." He keeps looking up across the hill, almost as though waiting for me to tell him which it is.

"To some it is death," I tell him.

We look at each other and I think for the first time we see each other as persons. Those eyes of his that are always darting about, impressing, commanding, selling, and making deals — those eyes are quiet in a face thoughtful and relaxed.

"We'll be missing you, Eric," he says. "You had more to teach us than I ever thought. I thank the Lord for showing me that before you left."

I watch his face and believe he is sincere. Tomorrow he will probably be rushing about again, making deals, pushing goods, and saving souls. But for one brief holy moment on this Christmas Day we are honest before each other. And I give thanks.

When everyone is gone, I watch Jim sweeping the walks on his way to the barn. The night is coming down across the hill, caressing the trees and hugging the snow. And I wait for the past to come back and visit us again. I wait for the sun to melt the snow and bring the hill to life. I wait to see three boys come romping down across the grass. I wait for the home Jim speaks of — the home where they worked and played and sang, close to parents, close to God, and just as happy as the grass was green.

But my waiting is wasted. The night keeps coming. The wind on the snow grows colder. And Jim is alone in the night.

My waiting is wasted. Home never comes. I thought perhaps it would. Perhaps this time I'd find it. But not tonight. Not here. And so I must be moving on.

14

"Why must you go, Eric?"

She asks it quietly, in a voice I've never heard
her use before. We stand in the snow, looking out
across Rabbit Lake, arms about each other, trying to
keep warm. Warm from the cold and warm from
good-bye. The old dilapidated building under the
trees sends us an apology for its sad-looking face.
There's a haunted touch to the place, just as Sara
said. Haunted and empty and godforsaken. A sign
proclaiming "U.S. Government" still hangs on the
gable end. Another newer sign hangs over the en-
trance below the faded one. "Jesus Saves" it says.
An English message for the Puerto Rican chapel.

"Does anyone ever know why he must move on,
Hazel?" I ask her, pulling her closer and kissing
her forehead.

She looks at me, her lovely eyes serious in the
afternoon light. It's the last day of the year, and as
December grinds out its final hours, we've come to
see the beautiful lake, to be alone, to have one last
happy time together before the train comes tonight
to carry Jim and me back to the city. Away from
Hazel and Eli and Wilmo and Rufus and all the

other dozens I've learned to know in these few short weeks. Away from innocence and peace. Away from a home where I was never quite born, a home that was here for Jim but not for me. Away. Back to the noise, the dirt, the slogans. Back to the world.

"I guess we're just a bunch of backward people," she sighs, her cheek pressed against my arm. There's a pouting in her comment, a disappointment, a solicitation.

"That's not fair, Hazel," I respond, my eyes intent on the water lapping at the ice's edge.

"But it's true, Eric. You've lived among us, trying to satisfy your fascination with a way of life that seems so foreign to the rest of your life. But now you've grown bored and restless and disappointed. So you're leaving." Her tone does not accuse or chasten. It begs for explanation.

What she says is true. I am restless to go. Somehow everything around here suddenly seems so unimportant, so irrelevant, so blandly ignorant of the larger world. The real world. The actual problems, the true causes, the real pains. The world has too many people, and these people act as though the divine purpose in marriage is having a dozen children or more. The atmosphere is breaking up, the fuel supplies are running low, and half the world is starving. And these people salve their consciences by sending missionaries to help while they themselves go on living as though nothing is happening. Nothing except maybe the end of the world.

But I am not bitter, not even angry. These people don't mean it evil-like. They truly do want to help.

140

Only their eyes have never been opened. And their faith teaches them that to see is sin. For didn't our first parents sin in order to have their eyes opened? If God wants us to see, He'll work the miracle.

"It's funny how I sort of thought you'd be here a longer time," she says. "I thought maybe one of these days you'd tell us about yourself, who you are, where you come from, and where you've been." I can feel her smiling against my shoulder, her soft dark hair pressed against my chin, her arm warm around my waist. "But I guess it's better this way. The truth might have made it hurt less."

"Hurt less?"

"Sure. You see, Eric, you know all about us. You've seen our good side and our bad side. You've been here long enough to measure us up, and you've found us wanting." She lifts her eyes to mine, a quiver passing imperceptibly through the soft skin of her beautiful face. "But you — we know almost nothing about you. You came from nowhere, and you're going back again. We know you're intelligent and friendly and gifted. We know that you can love and you can hate. But who are you, really? What makes you tick? What are you running from? And what are you really looking for? No one knows. No one knows because Eric has chosen not to tell us." Another quiver passes through her face as she looks up at me. "It seems unfair, but that's the way it is. And it's probably better for both of us."

"But you want it this way, don't you, Hazel?"

She nods, and I can feel her trembling in my arms as she pulls me close against her bosom, lifting closed eyes and a face burning with emotion, lips redder than the soft fabric of her dress. I kiss her gently, pulling her closer, our warm blood pulsating love through each other's veins. I kiss her again and again, our arms locking us into one as we stand there in the shadow of the haunted church, the wind sweeping the snow about us in a sort of ever-changing halo.

I can feel her tears hot on her face as her body sobs in my arms. She weeps without a sound and I kiss her over and over. Something deep, deep down in us is touching, and it touches for a long time. Something poetic, something violent and peaceful, something a lot of people never feel. Something neither of us understands.

The sun is falling behind the trees on the west bank of the lake when we reach the car. My arms are numb with cold, my toes freezing, but I hardly notice it. The warmth that passed between the two of us kept us from the cold. For this afternoon, at least.

We drive back past the little cabins in the snow, huddled together in the early evening, waiting for another year. Another year of hard work and laughter and poverty. Another year of slavery under the hot sun.

Hazel holds my hand in her lap, caressing it with her warm fingers. There's a contentedness in her face, and a new light in her eyes. Her dark hair falls loose about her face, her scarf pushed back around her neck. She lifts my cold hand to her lips and presses it against her cheek.

The radio in the old flipper doesn't amount to much, but it blares away with the top hits of the year that's just about to pull its curtains closed. The heater's warmer now and it's cozier in the old car. It's a precious moment as we lumber along the snowy roads on our way back to civilization.

Hazel brushes her hair back and fixes her scarf as we pass through the town. "Christmas lights are always sort of lonely on New Year's Eve," she says. "Somehow it seems darker than usual." She smiles. "I used to be scared to stay up and see the new year in. But Papa took me to church once long ago when I was young. There were lots of lights and we sang a lot. And Papa prayed the new year in." She laughs softly, musing to herself. "I've never been scared of it since then," she says.

We take the back way to her house so that we can drive through the old covered bridge. The moon has not come up yet and the ripples over the little falls above the bridge are dark against the snow. I turn down the radio and we listen to the wind singing against the wood of the old structure.

"Coming down this way at night always reminds me of the night Sara called and Papa and I came rushing over here to find her father hanging in the attic. It was really awful. Sara said she dreamed her father was going to the attic, yelling no one loved him and saying he was going to take his life. She said the dream must have wakened her and she went over to her parents' bedroom to quiet down. But her mother was alone, sleeping." Hazel pauses, her fingers digging deep into the palm of my hand as she remembers. "So Sara went to the attic and found him. It was a terrible sad thing."

We pass a mailbox as we make a turn in the road. "They live in there," she says. "Sara has survived better than I ever thought she would."

We come over the hill and the built-on sheds and the little house lie before us in the evening. Her fingers relax and she begins to stroke my hand again. "It's always good to come home," she says.

We sit in the car by the front gate, savoring our last aloneness together. There's a calmness between us, a quiet acceptance. "You know, Hazel," I say, "you are pretty much of a secret yourself."

"Why'd you say that?"

"What do I know about you, Hazel? What are you really like deep inside? What are you running from and where do you want to go? That part of you is as much a mystery as I am."

Laughing eyes watch me in the shadows. "That's what I meant," she says quietly in that voice with the playful, bursting quality. "The mystery would go away if we knew too much about each other."

"No, it wouldn't," I tell her, and I'm half shocked by my confession. I'm admitting that our warmth is more than fascination. It's much more subtle, much more genuine. And we both know it.

"Will you be coming back?" she asks.

"Maybe."

There are no more kisses, no more embraces, no hot tears or breaking tones, no more confessions. We sit for a long time, listening to the radio and watching the lights of her father's house. And then we go in.

"Where will you go next?" I ask her at the gate.

"Go?" The word falls toneless from her lips, her eyes emptied by the thought. "I won't go anyplace, Eric; this is home."

Inside, the sisters are getting supper. Eli sits by the stove, the Bible open in his lap, the telephone to his ear. His face is lined with fatigue.

"I'll be right over, Noah," he says. He listens. "Oh, that's okay, Noah," he says, his tone personal and sympathetic. "I'll help the boys get started with the feeding, and then I'll be right over. Hazel just came home, and she can help them till I get back."

Hazel hurries to the prophet's side as he hangs up. "What is it, Papa?"

"Noah Dombach's little Charity is quite sick again," he says. "The doctor says it's bad."

"Oh, the poor child. Won't she ever get well?"

Eli stands up and looks at his daughter. "If God wills it," he says.

"But, Papa, you're all played out and you have to speak at the watch-night service tonight. You should rest."

"Now, now, Hazel. Noah needs someone to stand by him. What if one of ours were sick?" He talks to her as though she were mother to the other eleven. And she is. This is indeed her home.

She takes my arm. "Eric has come to say good-bye, Papa."

He turns and walks toward me, his eyes searching my face. "I'm glad you came," he says.

"I am too."

The three of us are silent for a moment. It's the first I've spoken with Eli since that night almost three weeks ago when I went tearing out of here in the old flipper, angry about the veto of the play. The whole thing seems puny now. "I'm sorry," I say.

"I am too," he answers. He reaches out and shakes my hand. "I'm sorry you have to leave," he says. "You were such an inspiration to me."

I think of Ohio. I remember the Saturday mornings together. I remember those Sunday evenings, speaking at the same churches. And now here he stands, Bible in hand, dressed like a peasant, smelling like the barn, his face tired and worried about Noah's little girl.

"There's so much death," I say. "Don't you ever wish there'd be more birth and happiness?"

His answer is at once both firm and gentle. "Death and birth aren't all that different, Eric, if we believe in God."

It's his last word of faith to me. I shake his hand and thank him for everything. I give Hazel my last smile. And as I walk toward the door, something passes from me.

I turn and look back at them, together in the pale light of their humble home. There's a kiss on Hazel's lips as she watches me, a kiss and a thank-you. She knows I'll never be back. But Eli isn't sure. "God go with you," he calls. "And remember, never settle for anything less."

And then I go. I've been going for several weeks now, pulling myself away bit by bit. But it isn't easy. It's hard to believe that I've become so attached to these people in such a short time.

The radio in the kitchen is playing gospel music from a local "religious" station when I get back to the Witmers. The milking finished early, Wilmo has put on a clean shirt and he sits at the table, talking to Anna as she dishes the meal. Menno relaxes in his rocker, his head deep in the afghan.

"But someone ought to go over there and help Noah," the hired man is saying. "It sounds pretty bad, doesn't it, Anna?"

"Yes, Bertha made it sound very serious," she says. "They say there's no cure for it, you know."

Wilmo nods. "Charity's a cute little child," he says. "I sure hope she doesn't die."

Menno clears his throat. "Maybe you and I should go on over there after we drop the boys off at the station."

"I'll send some cookies along," Anna says.

It's a big meal. My favorite. Ham loaf. Ham loaf with lots of peas and noodles and homemade bread.

Jim and I go upstairs to the big empty bedroom and carry down our baggage. I have to make a second trip to get all my things and I hurry, anxious to flee from the high ceiling and the dark corners of the room big enough for three. Three gone away, one by one.

Anna doesn't say much as the farmers put on their coats and hats and help us carry our things to the door. "Come and see us as often as you can," she says. But a reservation in her eyes makes me wonder how much she really means it. What she really wants to tell me is to bring her James home to her as often as I can. But I take no offense. She's been wonderful, really. In her own unique way, she's shown more interest in me than my own mother has.

"Thanks for everything, Mrs. Witmer. I'll make sure he writes every week." She smiles and Jim smiles. There is no kiss, no good-bye. But the smile is enough.

"I'll try to do better, Mom," he says. "Please don't work so hard. You and Pop gotta learn to take it easy."

She's still smiling when we turn to go. I think I shall always remember her that way. A slow smile etched in the serious face of a mother who has surrendered two of her boys to the hill. And the world is beckoning the third.

I take one last look at the hill, formless and mute in the night. The snow is still there.

The ticket clerk tells us the train will be late. Terrific. We're liable to see the new year in, stranded on the cold tracks halfway between Trenton and Newark.

Menno is even less emotional about good-byes than his wife. "We enjoyed your visit." And to his son, "Be careful, James. And write to your mother."

He turns and walks away, leaving us in the chilly station with our earthly goods at our feet. Wilmo lags behind, reading the train notices taped on the wall.

"I think I'll miss you," he says to me, almost apologetically. "Thanks for the toolbox."

And then he too is gone. And as before, Jim and I are alone in a dark empty place.

15

Once again, a filthy car, one moment hot, one moment cold. And a grumpy conductor. Jim and I turn the seat in front of us around so that we can put our feet up and relax. "Feet off the seats," barks the conductor. Which would be okay, except the seat's dirtier than my shoes.

"If you want to be jolted back to the real world," Jim says to me after the old man leaves the car, "just take the train. Even in the daytime, when I can see the quiet country outside, I get this paranoia as soon as I get on the train. Everyone shouts and acts as though I'm trying to take advantage of them." He chuckles. "All I'm trying to do is get a ride back to the city."

"Yeah, it's almost as bad as the subway."

We ride in silence most of the way to Philadelphia. Jim dozes off and I try to catch up on the recent news, reading a magazine I find on the seat across the aisle. Seems like a lot has happened. My news habits have sort of fallen apart. It used to be my big thing at school. I even did some reporting one summer for a newspaper downtown. But world affairs lost their importance on the farm. No one at Green

Thumb had the slightest idea what was really happening in the Middle East or Vietnam, let alone the military intelligence in this country. Marriages were the big news. And once in a while someone held up a gas station and made off with twenty-five dollars and thirty-four cents. Everyone was shocked. Man, in New York people are murdered, legally and illegally, all over the place and the *Times* doesn't even print their obituaries. But that's the difference, I guess. The difference between here and there. And I'm in between.

An old church spire looms high in the skyline as we crawl into Philadelphia. Another dark city, already half drunk from singing the old year out. And the spire overlooks it all.

Jim jerks awake. "Boy, what a letdown," he says. "I was dreaming I was home." He rubs his eyes.

"And where was that?" I ask.

He looks at me. "I don't want to talk about it anymore." There's resentment in his voice.

"Why not, Jim?"

"Because I think you're being cynical."

I watch the church spire glide away as the train starts moving again. So he thinks I'm cynical. Wow. You love a place; you try to be accepted and discover it's impossible. So you go back to where you started — which isn't much now that Big John's gone. And that's what he calls cynical?

"I'm sorry if I sounded that way, Jim. I'm not. I am a little sad, a little confused, and a little disappointed. But I'm not cynical. I learned too much for that."

His eyes are gentle. As usual, like Jim. "You know I appreciate what you've done," he says.

I nod.

"But it just doesn't figure, Eric. You stay there with my parents, you cut your hair and join the church, you get a job and apparently fall in love with one of our most sought after young girls. But when Christmas comes, you suddenly pull stakes and drop it all."

"I know." How can I explain it? Jim is so close to me, almost a brother. But we're strangers at heart. The wandering in my blood, the lack of roots that's always seeking them, the whole world to discover with no one to anchor me. This Jim doesn't comprehend. So he can't put it all together — that I met God in Eli, that I'll never be the same because of it, that I met God in Rufus, too, late on Christmas afternoon. That a part of me seeks to open cages, and shout freedom to the prisoners we all create, and praise God. And yet I must wander.

There's so much to talk about, now that we're gone. But I don't know how to say it without sounding stupid and insulting.

"Believe me, Jim, I wish I could live like them. But I've seen too much of the rest of the world."

He smiles. "I'm not for a moment asking you to be like them, Eric. I myself have chosen to struggle with the larger world. But each time I go home, I have this feeling that they in their own small world have discovered as much of the heart of living as I have."

"Jim, I agree with you. But I just saw it wasn't my bag. I must live my own life and find my own

151

home. But that doesn't mean I'll forget Hazel and Eli and Rufus and your folks and all the rest. I won't."

We're more like brothers again, and I take out my guitar and we sing for a while. The car is dismal and deserted; so we sing as loud as we wish. And there's peace in our song. Peace and acceptance of distance between.

"You think you'll go back?" he asks, dark hair hanging in his eyes as he slouches beside me, feet up on the seat again.

I play another piece or two before I answer, listening to the song of the weary rails and thinking it over.

"No, Jim, I doubt that I'll ever go back. It's better remembered than visited now."

"And Hazel?"

"She'll always be there. But she won't be waiting for me. She'll get married one of these days, and she'll be a good Mennonite woman. Oh, occasionally she'll cause a stir. But she's like a mother to your people — she's always protecting them and taking care. Just like she does to her own brothers and sisters. But me — if I'd go back, she'd deny we'd ever been friends. That's just the way she is."

"John used to talk about marrying her and bringing her to the city. Back when we first went to college." He chuckles.

"And you, Jim, did you think it was a good idea?"

"Hazel and I never got along," he says. "I guess I always tried too hard to figure her out. She isn't the kind that goes for that."

We think a while, each mile carrying us further

from that place of childhood and innocence. "I think I'll miss Eli most of all," I say. And it's true. Eli is a great man. Wise and humble and full of God.

The train stops at Trenton a little after eleven. Two pretty black girls get on, heavy in conversation with a male voice that sounds suddenly familiar. I turn and look at them as they toss sleeping bags and suitcases into the empty seats. I nudge Jim.

"Hey, doesn't that look like Wilson? I can't tell with that hat he's wearing."

He looks. "Yeah. But I can't really tell. You know him better than I do."

I watch them sit down, the three of them in two seats, talking loud and fast as though they've had a little too much celebrating. Then he sees me.

"Hey, Eric baby!" he calls, swearing as he crawls out of their laps. "What you doing on this train, man?"

I jump up and meet him halfway back the aisle as he puts his arms around me in a big theatrical hug. "How you doing, Wilson?" I ask.

"How'm I doing, huh?" He turns to the girls in mock exasperation. "Listen to the man. He wants to know, on a great night like this, how I'm doing!" He rolls his eyes. "Shame, shame, shame, Eric. You oughta be ashamed of yourself, you oughta." He pulls a bottle from his pocket, takes a drink, and hands it to me. "Come on, man, join the celebration."

"No, thanks, Wilson, not now. Maybe later."

He shrugs. "Whatever you say. Say, you want to meet some real sexy women? Let me have the honor of introducing Jennie and Liz."

153

They smile. "Revolutionaries?" I ask.

"Oh, sure, Eric. These chicks know where it's at, man. We spent the whole vacation together. Didn't we?"

Jennie wets her lips as she smiles voluptuously. "Oh, baby, the Revolution is hot and groovy." All three laugh uproariously. It's a familiar scene grown suddenly strange.

"Man, I haven't seen you around much since the take-over. Where you been keeping yourself?"

I look at him as he hands the bottle to the girls. What does one say to a former friend who used to have no time for women because he was bent on changing the world? The Revolution ran in his veins and he and Big John were always out there socking it to them. Quoting Marx and Che and Lenin, roaring at the kids and roaring at the cops.

Now he stands beside me in the empty car, all decked out in a silly paper hat and cheap horn to trumpet in the new day, half drunk, sexed out, and grinning like an old retarded bum fleeing the disillusionment of a day gone by.

"I went to help bury Big John," I tell him.

The grin goes from his teeth and the wrinkles leave his dark skin sober for a moment. "Big John?" he asks.

"Yeah, Wilson, Big John."

His eyes watch me. Then he lets out a roar of awful laughter and rolls back into the seats, his clenched fists raised in a terrible hysteria as his mind fights off the truth of what he's seen in my face. His laughter becomes a scream of anguish as the girls unknowingly

154

join in the frightening song of death, gleefully pulling his body against their own in a double caress. The whole thing writhes on my brain like a horrible slow motion film of human agony, three children laughing themselves to death, a young broken man wrestling with his sorrow in the senseless arms of his mistresses, drunk and confused and alone in the last hour of the day.

I wander back to Jim and slump in my seat, afraid. Afraid and alone. To Jim and his people there was so much I could never explain. And now the world I knew so well has become foreign too. Wilson would never understand where I've been these weeks, what I've seen and felt, and how I've changed.

And so the train goes on. Between here and there, between then and now. And I am in between.

"It's midnight," Jim says as the Manhattan skyline comes into view.

"It sure is," I say, settling back, waiting to feel a new year come rushing by. But there is nothing. Nothing but the song of the rails and the cheap junky horns of Wilson and his friends.

And then we are there. The escalator isn't working; so we lug our stuff up the narrow stairs. The station looms all about us, full of people in weird costumes and those awful horns.

"You going to the campus?" Jim asks when we stop to rest.

"I don't know where I'm going, Jim. Maybe I'll try to finish school; maybe I won't. Maybe I'll even go off. to the war."

His face is open, sincere. "I think I'll go back

to my room," he says. "I think I'll try to start the new year by keeping a promise to my mother."

"You mean you're going to write your mother a letter tonight yet?"

"Sure, Eric. There's never a better time to write home than when you've just been there."

We shake hands again and say our thanks. And then we part. Without a word. He takes a bus and I stumble over to the subway, trying to decide if I want to go back to that empty room. The air is cold in the underground.

The train screeches in and I scramble on, pulling my baggage with me. And then it lurches forward into the night.

At the 42nd Street stop the crowd comes pushing on, fresh from the mob in Times Square. They push and shove and yell as they move into the car, packing us body to body, flesh to flesh, like cattle sardined in a butcher's pen. I hold my guitar over my head so that it won't get crushed as they push me against a seat full of more people in silly hats. I can't move and my suitcase is gone. I want to shout at the mob, but they couldn't hear me above the din. So I just grit my teeth and stare at the admonition on the wall in front of me, warning me not to litter, smoke, or spit.

And then we're off again. Me and the world. To the tune of the rail. Caught between a day that's going and a day that's coming. Caught. And alone and afraid.